**VULTURES
OF PARADISE**

Also by the same author

Oxygen Manifesto: A Battle for the Environment

VULTURES OF PARADISE

Atulya Misra

Published by
Rupa Publications India Pvt. Ltd 2021
7/16, Ansari Road, Daryaganj
New Delhi 110002

Sales centres:
Allahabad Bengaluru Chennai
Hyderabad Jaipur Kathmandu
Kolkata Mumbai

Copyright © Atulya Misra 2021

This is a work of fiction. Names, characters, places and incidents are either the product of the author's imagination or are used fictitiously and any resemblance to any actual person, living or dead, events or locales is entirely coincidental.

All rights reserved.

No part of this publication may be reproduced, transmitted, or stored in a retrieval system, in any form or by any means, electronic, mechanical, photocopying, recording or otherwise, without the prior permission of the publisher.

ISBN: 978-93-91256-63-0

Second impression 2021

10 9 8 7 6 5 4 3 2

The moral right of the author has been asserted.

Printed at Parksons Graphics Pvt. Ltd., Mumbai

This book is sold subject to the condition that it shall not, by way of trade or otherwise, be lent, resold, hired out, or otherwise circulated, without the publisher's prior consent, in any form of binding or cover other than that in which it is published.

*Dedicated to my two lovely daughters,
Indrani and Ishita*

Contents

1.	Black 'n' White	1
2.	Feast of the Vultures	14
3.	Sridhar—The Solitary Seeker	38
4.	Brigette—The Sculptor of Destiny	47
5.	Theatre of the Absurd	63
6.	The Flying Carpet	71
7.	Life's Eternal Cycle	85
8.	Rolled in Hot Furnaces—Steel	92
9.	Tower of Silence	104
10.	Wealth from Waste	115
11.	African Adventure	130
12.	The Waste Factory	154
13.	A Paradise Reneged	164
14.	Tandav—The Dance of Shiva	180
15.	Pandora's Box	192
16.	Return to Paradise	205
Acknowledgements		211

1

Black 'n' White

It was turning cold in the island of Ibiza. Roneo had finished work and was ready to head home. As usual, Roneo made his last call to Rebecca. After four long beeps, as expected, it went to the answering machine and typically, he did not leave a message.

Things were no longer the same between him and Rebecca. They had come to Ibiza to escape, to rejuvenate their stale lives and later, to return to live their lives as per their original design, their original dreams.

He now worked part-time for *Ibiza Life,* a weekly magazine covering events in the party town. This provided him with a meagre income. In his leisure time, he freelanced to augment his measly earnings. Rebecca worked as a salesperson in a supermarket. Roneo's work started after dusk, while Rebecca had to be ready by dawn to be on time for her shift. After an early dinner and a glass of wine, they would try to find the time to get into bed together. After a bout of physical intimacy—kissing, caressing and the occasional lovemaking—they would grab a nap. Romeo would then quickly get dressed, pull on his photographer's jacket, pick up his camera bag, give Rebecca a goodnight kiss, switch the lights off and head out. Very often, he would return only a few moments later to pick up his press ID, his scooter keys or his wallet and then would hurriedly rush out again, waking up half the neighbourhood in his haste. Rebecca would pretend to be asleep, and after he left, she would struggle to sleep. She would wake up all groggy and would rush to the supermarket before sunrise.

Roneo's work started around midnight, when the party spots, bars and beaches would start buzzing with all the happening people. All through the night, he was kept busy, clicking photograph after photograph. Candid shots of the rich and the well-heeled, dressed in the latest fashions in chic restaurants and bars, smiling faces and dancing feet. These photographs, which depicted certain specified moods, created a thrill and brought back clusters of the posh to the premises, night after night.

He would return home to catch up with Rebecca, but more often than not, he would find her almost ready to leave for work. After spending the entire forenoon in bed, sleeping like a log, he would rush to the magazine office to submit his work and be assigned his beat for the upcoming evening. Part-timers like Roneo were paid based on published material. He had to often scurry from one office to another to get timely payments. He would again rush back in the evening, hoping to be home before Rebecca arrived. Often, he would find her already there, exhausted, fast asleep without even having changed out of her uniform. He would make her a coffee and order dinner from an outlet nearby or otherwise make some eggs and toast.

Rebecca hated her job as a sales staff member. She hated

smiling at unknown faces, sorting items during lean hours, counting cash and managing unruly customers who kept complaining of long rows, delays at the counters, stale items or who kept demanding to exchange goods. It was not in her nature to be polite and smiling all the time, but it was a requirement of the job.

On most days of the week, life was an unending drudgery for them. They worked like machines and ended up hurling their frustrations at each other. During the weekends, Rebecca wanted Roneo to be with her. But for Roneo, weekends were busy with back-to-back parties; that's when the islanded paradise was in full swing.

On Tuesdays, he was often free; he had no assignments lined up as that was the only day with very few parties scheduled and Ibiza took a moment to breathe before the pandemonium continued. Roneo would make breakfast for Rebecca and visit her at the supermarket during her lunch break. Lately, he had begun to work on Tuesdays too. And if he had no assignments, he would sleep endlessly, as if to cover up for his weekly sleep deficit.

Roneo avoided fights with Rebecca; whenever he sensed a fight brewing, he went mum. He gradually reconciled to his fate and had started to learn how to live like a freelance photojournalist of little consequence, rather than the ace wildlife photographer he once dreamt of being. Rebecca had also more or less forgotten all her dreams and her desires to become a fashion model. She had started to accept her dull, dreary existence as a supermarket salesperson: selling clothes, cosmetics, grocery and other household items to people, most of whom were old and had all the time in the world to while away at the store, amidst countless items imported from China and other parts of the world to fill their tiny houses. Roneo and Rebecca lived this meaningless life for days, for months and for years, while the swish set from around the world partied and had fun in Ibiza.

Roneo had expected much in his youth. He was from an alpine village in northern Spain where the summers were cold and the winters harsh and unbearable. His family grew olives and also reared ducks and sheep. Occasionally, he used to go hunting in the forests that dotted the slopes of the hills. The Communist party had grown its support base amongst the peasants in his alpine village. All the landlords, petty traders, factory owners and the rich and the powerful had either been driven away from the countryside or were killed. The Communist party's armed ruffians would frequently descend on the villages up north to line up, kill and then to cart away the corpses of their so-called opponents of the revolution in clumsy lorries to be dumped in mass graves. His uncle, George, was considered a Communist sympathiser and thus, his family was considered safe. Nevertheless, there were Communists within Communists, power groups within power groups, power grabbers within leaders, which made everybody safe yet vulnerable at the same time. This phase ended when power was consolidated in their hands and the populace's spirit for reprisal were exhausted, extinguished and tamed.

He and his uncle were the best of buddies.

After spending his mornings at school, he would help his family in the olive fields—plucking and drying the fruits and then passing them through a cold press to collect the virgin oil. Once the first harvest of virgin oil was complete, more oil was extracted by cold and hot presses to get other grades, which finally left them with waste to use as cattle feed. On weekends and holidays, he went deep into the forest with his uncle and other cousins to

hunt. Roneo never liked to kill and so, Uncle George bought him a box camera—'Made in East Germany'. Roneo discovered that he had a passion for photography. He soon became engrossed in taking pictures of flowers, butterflies with intricate wings, birds with colourful feathers and animals with beautiful fur. Many a time, the creature he had photographed alive would be killed by a gang of poachers soon after. He never took pictures of lifeless hunted animals with pain in their dead eyes.

Soon after high school, Roneo decided to pursue photography as a career. With the help of his uncle, he was able to gain admission in a school of fine arts that had recently introduced photography as a stream. The fees were affordable since in the Communist regime, education was highly subsidized. Roneo also managed to get a scholarship, which helped sustain his stay in Madrid in a shared apartment. The more he learnt about filters, lenses, lights and equipment, the more he found himself engrossed and passionate about photography. Soon, he scrimped and saved to buy himself a Russian-made Zenit camera, a variety of lenses, flashes and a sturdy tripod. After classes, he would venture into the city gardens to take photographs of nature's marvels. On weekends, he would go to the zoo or trek deep into the forests to spot animals, birds, trees or for that matter, any element of nature that grabbed his interest.

Most evenings, Roneo would be in the lab, developing his black and white negatives. As rolls were very expensive, he had learnt to sit patiently, and to press the shutter at the right moment. As a child, he was intrigued by his grandfather, patiently sitting by the river with his fishing tackle to catch something. The old man and his friends would sit silently, patiently, motionlessly for hours to get their catch. Later they would rejoice and cook their combined catch for supper. Roneo too would sit still, hidden and alone for hours to capture a jumping squirrel or a bear playing with his cubs in his frame. He painstakingly created albums: pasting his prized photographs on black paper with white paper frames, interspersing a muslin translucent sheet between the pictures. He saved the negatives in airtight boxes as trophies, or for future use.

Roneo's photographs started getting printed in the school's journals and sometimes, even in the propaganda souvenirs of the Communist party that depicted the beauty of Spain's countryside. Roneo was beginning to be recognised as an emerging photographer of the school.

However, things changed very rapidly in the political horizon. The Communist party was losing ground, and the liberal democrats quickly buried them in the graveyards of history. Democracy, freedom and market economy became the new buzzwords. Government grants to liberal arts schools were curtailed and students were persuaded to take loans for education as scholarships no longer existed.

Technological advances and the advent of colour photography pushed Roneo to buy a Nikon camera at an exorbitant price, further undermining his precarious position. The rolls had to now be developed in labs, using state-of-the-art machines, making it expensive and with little elbow space left for corrections during processing. To get a photograph that could pay the bills, one needed expensive equipment and deep pockets.

He started buying rolls with higher ASA to get better results for action and dim lights. Roneo became a master of combining ASA, shutter speed, lenses and filters to get photographs of his choice.

However within no time, equipment became more valued than skill. The autofocus models made it possible for even a novice to capture a moment. Now, the camera automatically selected an appropriate aperture and shutter speed all by itself.

Roneo was shaken out of his reverie. It was past 1 a.m. when the party ended abruptly. One of the party animals had collapsed due to exhaustion on the dance floor, leading to a commotion and successive dispersal of the lingering crowd to other locations. Roneo spent some time with the bartender. He had no other destination on his beat that night. Instead of driving into his apartment parking lot on his scooter, waking up the entire neighbourhood and disturbing a sleeping Rebecca who had to be awake again at 5 a.m. for her shift at the store, he decided to take a walk on the beach.

He put his backpack down on the glistening sand and stretched himself out. The cool breeze, the sound of the gushing waves and the moonlit sand refreshed him after his tiring day. He lay there motionless for some time, with his head resting on the cushy backpack.

Later he took off his shoes, rolled up his trousers to his knees and walked leisurely on the wet sand. There was nobody around. For a moment, he felt as if the entire planet was his alone. Then he looked up at the sky, the moon, the twinkling stars, the push-and-pull of the dark huge ocean in front of him, the quietness and the stillness... and felt contained within the cosmos. He had not had such feelings for a very long time; it had been so long since he had been in the wild, since he had felt that he was one with nature!

Was he hallucinating?

The clubs and the bars that he frequented for work was filled with smoke from weed and drugs. Was he high owing to passive smoke clusters or was it the two complimentary shots of vodka the bartender had poured for him just before the bar closed? Whatever it was, he was feeling good after a long, long time.

In the distance, he spotted two bare bodies. They were moving. Two nude girls were dancing on the beach as if they owned the moment. He was not alone.

Someone else owned the planet now, and he felt like a tenant. They looked so beautiful! So ethereal and otherworldly, their beautiful bodies swaying sensuously on glistening sands under the milky moon, with waves crashing on the shore behind them! Were they angels? He had to capture them before they realised that he was there. He fell softly to the sands, and reached for his equipment, which was in his backpack, slowly crawling forward on all fours. He found a hiding place behind a tree trunk not far from where they swayed.

In no time, Roneo had set up his tripod and his camera and started clicking shot after shot. Dancing fairies, laughing fairies and fairies in embrace. It was quite a spectacle. He took hundreds of photographs in quick succession. He tried out various apertures and shutter speeds; he changed his lenses often to get wide angles and telescopic shots. The fairies had now settled down, and so did he. The dark sky was giving way to an orange flush in the azure sky, indicating the arrival of the sun. Roneo packed his equipment and lit a cigarette where he sat. He saw the fairies beating a hasty retreat on the other side of the horizon.

When Roneo reached home, Rebecca was getting ready to leave for work. He did not bother to make himself breakfast. He was too sleepy. He slept like a log until hunger and dehydration

got him up on his feet. After gulping down a cup of coffee and a cold sandwich at the gas station, he knocked on the door of the editor's cabin. After showing him the regular photographs of nightlife, the bands, the restaurants and the discos, he testily dropped his voice to a low. In an icy and steely tone he told the editor about his 'extra-terrestrial encounter'.

The editor was not too impressed. Nudes were, after all, not uncommon in Ibiza; in fact, they were a dime a dozen. His magazine had a limited aim—to promote life in Ibiza and get paid for the promotions. The restaurants and bars regularly paid the magazine. A picture of two nude women dancing on the beach would invite no fresh eyes and thus could be given no space in his magazines. However, he looked at the photographs, just out of curiosity. After all, he was a man!

After glancing, then poring through them, he stayed glued and realised that they were not the regular kind of nudes lying bare to offer cheap thrills. There was something special about the photographs. They were neither vulgar nor sexual. They were spontaneous and yet outright artistic. The photographs had tremendous intensity, beauty and splendour. They were art, tantalising art.

These ethereal photographs deserved so much more than just to be published in a magazine!

The editor selected a few of the photographs and kept them aside for an appraisal at the next editorial meeting. However, he kept his plans to himself. He told Roneo that this work was of no use for his magazines. He told him that he sold products, not fairies. And that, anyway, his magazine was not a *Playboy* or a *Penthouse*, to be featuring nudes. Roneo left the office devastated.

Roneo never discussed his work with Rebecca, not since

they had moved to Ibiza. It made him feel small, ashamed and disgusted. This was not what he had set out to do. He had dreamt of becoming a wildlife photographer and now, he was a common paparazzi, making money by photographing meaningless parties, people, restaurants and bars.

The same was true for Rebecca. She hated her job. It was so worthless and boring. She was not cut out to be working at a store, pandering to cranky customers. She had always dreamt of being a model, of living a glamorous life, but that seemed like a distant dream. Now, all she could do was wait, wait endlessly... she too was ashamed to discuss her work with Roneo. It was with him that she had dreamt her ambitious dreams and talking about them made her dreams drift further away.

Nonetheless, that day, Roneo showed his photographs to Rebecca. 'Since when have you gotten into shooting pornography?' was her first reaction. But then, suddenly, Rebecca paused and looked at the photographs again. Her eyes widened and she exclaimed, 'These... are works of art. They are wonderful, Roneo. You deserve shots like these. They look like angels. One of them is so much like us. The other one is so unusually sublime—a pure beauty. It is a masterpiece. Don't waste these in that promotional magazine of yours. These photographs will give you what you have been aspiring for all these years. They will put you in the big league and give you the name and fame you have always deserved.'

Roneo rushed back to the editor to retrieve the photographs. However, the editor informed him that *The New York Times* had already purchased them. He proudly said, 'Your pieces will feature in the most acclaimed newspaper in the world—in its art segment. It might already have gone into print. You have

now made a formidable name for yourself. These photographs will take you places.'

'Is there any way to retrieve them first?' asked Roneo surprised. 'We need to take permission from the women we have featured in the photos. That is our work ethic.'

'You should have done due diligence before bringing them to me, Roneo. Anyway, angels do not give permission to anybody. You may have to search for them in the heavens. The photograph will make them famous. They will always owe us a favour. So, don't worry and go and get some rest. Tomorrow will not be the same as today. Roneo, your days of anonymity seem to be over,' the editor added.

The next day, Roneo was hastily woken up by a dozen uniformed men who had already ransacked his entire house before turning him over from his deep slumber. It was five in the evening and Rebecca would be returning home in an hour; he also needed to get ready for work. Maybe these people knew about his accomplishment? Maybe he was already a celebrity?

But looking at their uniform and the method in their madness it was obvious that these men meant business. They started packing all his equipment, negatives, photographs, and his computer, printer, tripods and other equipment neatly in strong steel boxes and sealing them with duct tape. Even his personal belongings—all his albums, his files, certificates, medals and documents were being sealed in boxes.

'What is all this happening here? Who are you guys?' he asked, rather alarmed. 'You can't take all this away. This is my work and my source of livelihood.'

'We are not here to steal. We are here for a deal,' said one of them as he threw a blank cheque towards Roneo. 'Write down whatever amount you wish as barter. As of now you are also on the wrong side of the law for breaching privacy, so this should be worth your while.'

Roneo was suddenly afraid. He was reminded of his poverty, his loans and his desire to make Rebecca happy. Together they could have achieved so much more if they had enough money. What if he had to attend to a long-drawn legal battle and the spectre of imprisonment over these pictures?

After some mental calculations, Roneo wrote out a figure on the cheque, knowing fully well that it would be too good a bargain. The head of the dirty dozen smiled. He suffixed another zero to what Roneo had been aspiring for. After a little thought, he made a brief phone call and placed another zero on the pre-signed cheque. Roneo was a hundred times richer than what he could have possibly ever envisaged. The dirty dozen bade him goodbye, as they loaded his personal effects into a van and left .

Rebecca soon returned home. She was shocked to see the ransacked house. But Roneo smiled happily and waved the cheque at her, telling her that it was their passport to the world of their dreams.

Roneo found it hard to reach the editor. After many attempts, he managed to get him on the phone. The editor said, 'The girls you photographed were neither fairies nor angels. They were princesses. Now forget what we all did for our living. It is time to walk on the clouds.'

Roneo now knew that the dirty dozen had already taken care of the editor before coming to his house. He and Rebecca hurriedly packed the rest of their things, jumped into a cab and drove down to the ferry station to catch a boat. They would head to the mainland. From Barcelona, they took a flight to finally

return to Madrid to restart their lives from where they had left. Yes, they were ready to start afresh...

The newspapers from the United States arrived to stand in other countries with a time lag. *The New York Times* that weekend had no arts section. The section had been withdrawn in the international edition. In the United States too, most of the copies were mysteriously picked up before daybreak. For many years to come, Roneo never saw what he had photographed that night.

Who were these angels who had suddenly appeared and who had returned to him all that he had lost? Who had given him and Rebecca a fresh start? Roneo often thought of those princesses and wondered why they had come to Ibiza on that fateful night. Where had they come from?

It was time to move on. Roneo got ready for an assignment which soon turned into an escapade.

2

Feast of the Vultures

Nobody knew the exact date and time of Hirachand's birth. At best, it was known that he was born the year Gadar Khan visited their house in Hisar, bringing messages of the revolt against foreign rulers, written and baked in rotis -Indian breads, before he was caught by the Company's sepoys. He, with his three accomplices, were killed, and their naked bodies were left hanging on a neem tree close to his own fields. They were later thrown into an irrigation canal, which flowed not very far from their town.

The shadow of treachery loomed large over his family for allegedly helping the European company locate Gadar Khan, one of the heroes of the first war of independence fought against the East India Company, in a bid to restore the crown to a disillusioned, ageing and poetry-loving Mughal emperor; a man who was destined to be the last in line of the Mughal dynasty. Soon the revolt was quelled and the emperor, his youngest wife and two of her sons were exiled to Rangoon; the family covered thousands of miles in a caravan of bullock carts. Here they lived for many years under house arrest on a meagre pension. The rest of the Mughals were killed and hung in various places in the walled city, many of them at the Khooni Darwaza in the Mughal capital city of Delhi. The youngest queen and her two sons were spared, as they had clandestinely supported the English regent. The British queen, who took over the crown soon after, was very particular that the emperor be pardoned and not given the death penalty as a matter of royal privilege.

Hirachand's family got some of their lost glory back when a sparsely clad Mahatma from Gujarat visited their home briefly, while touring the nation to spread the message of self-assertion and home rule.

As his demand for goat milk could not be fulfilled by the Hindu merchant households, it had to be procured from a man named Mustafa, living in a Muslim neighbourhood. Mustafa renamed his three-year-old son Imran as Gandhi Qureshi to mark this historic event!

Hirachand was married off to Kalawati even before he had reached the age of ten. His wife, however, could not join him after the mandatory *gauna* (conjugation) ceremony as her whole village was wiped out by the plague. The entire population of the village either succumbed to the dreaded disease or ran for their lives to far-flung places. The health office burned all their huts and belongings to prevent the spread of the epidemic. Nobody knew if Kalawati had survived the ordeal. Later, to mock Hirachand, people carried tales of her being spotted in old Delhi's mujaras or dancing houses. Later, Hirachand was married again. His second wife, Padma, reached puberty after a short separation, a little after their marriage. She however died during labour, becoming a statistic in the growing list of maternal fatalities. Hirachand was lucky in his third marriage to Meenakshi, with whom he had eight boys and four girls in quick succession. Hirachand named all his daughters after rivers—from Indu in the west, Ganga in the north, Narmada in central India to Cauvery in the south—across the length and breadth of India. With regard to his sons, Hirachand preferred to name them after gemstones. From Moti to Panna to Neelam; bearing astrological significance devoted to leading stars. His youngest son was born sixty years after the Great Indian Revolt. This slight misadventure was blamed on the power of the planet Mars, and the outstanding beauty of Meenakshi, who always remained veiled. Hirachand named his youngest son after the stone signifying his rising star, the Sun, and called him Manikchand, before taking a vow of celibacy to prevent any such further accidents. In any case, he now already had a flourishing family of sons, daughters, granddaughters and great grandsons.

Manikchand was an intelligent child with a natural aptitude for numbers. He was also well-built and taller than most children of his age. Hirachand had him admitted in the village primary school, and he always topped his class. On the advice of the teachers, Hirachand permitted him to join middle school, which was situated in a village cluster some eight miles from where they lived. This school catered to some hundred villages around the cluster. Each day, Manikchand woke up early and walked to the school, crossing the village paths, bullock cart trails and pebbled streets to reach the motorable road on which the school stood. On the way, he had to cross a temple devoted to Narad Muni. A drinking water well, an old banyan tree and a cement-paved sitting area marked the spot. He often sat in the temple courtyard to pray, rest and sometimes, to finish his homework.

Many a times, students from the other villages also gathered at the temple and Manikchand would join them. They would go together to school, running, shouting, teasing, swiping at each other and cracking jokes about the teachers.

Manikchand was one of the best students in his class. Only one other student hailing from another far-flung village consistently outperformed him.

Gulveer Chaudhary was outstanding. He scored the highest, in every subject taught in the school, with ease. He was muscular and handsome, and highly charismatic. Gulveer was able to influence everybody around him. He always ran through the school gates wearing a broad smile and was kind and helpful to the other students, especially those who struggled with their studies. He seemed to know almost everything. Gulveer narrated tales of the young revolutionaries of Punjab who wanted to free India from the British rule, to other students of the school.

Manikchand and Gulveer hit it off immediately and became great friends. Soon, they were joined at the hip. When the great revolutionary Bhagat Singh was given capital punishment, they wanted to run away from home to become freedom fighters and fight against the foreign rulers. They learnt the anthems of independence and often sang them aloud to the school's consternation. The school discouraged open support to the freedom struggle, although most of the teachers were nationalists at heart. Manikchand was only second to Gulveer in class, because he too was an exceptionally bright student. But Gulveer had mesmerised him with his intellect, patriotic fervour, resilience, helpful nature, easy-going attitude and above all, with the stories he knew and the songs that he sung.

Gulveer lived in Jat Tola, some ten miles from the school,

towards Kurukshetra. The Jats, who often lived in single community habitations, were one of the most hardworking communities in the region. They were masters of agriculture, and even women joined the men in the fields. They toiled in harsh soils and difficult terrain and were successful in garnering very good yields from the land. The men and women were tall, fair and handsome. Once, centuries ago, they had inhabited the plains of Doab, after descending from the regions near the Caspian Sea through the upper-Himalayas and the Mediterranean, bringing with them their pastoral culture and intensive agricultural practices. They transformed the region into the largest provider of wheat, pulses, fodder, sugarcane and oil seeds, in addition to fruits, vegetable, milk and milk products.

Manikchand passed his seventh grade examinations with flying colours, just a few marks behind Gulveer in each subject. In the education system introduced by Lord Macaulay, only highly intelligent and extremely hardworking students could move ahead after middle school. Most jobs, including that of teachers, only required a middle pass certificate as the mandatory qualification. Inter-colleges were only present in a few large cities called commissionaires. The student who topped middle school in the region, where Manikchand lived, would get admission to the inter-college in the town of Rohtak.

For Manikchand, topping the school became an obsession. He realised that it would be his ticket to success in life. He would be eligible for any job of his choice. He could possibly even get a chance to become a graduate. Being a graduate could make him a 'bara sahib' and afford him the opportunity to rub shoulders with the British bosses. The only hurdle was Gulveer, his best friend and idol who had always been ahead of him in the race.

One day, Manikchand reached the Narad Muni temple a little early. Manikchand prayed to Narad Muni for his success. The deity has a unique status in Hindu mythology. Narad Muni is an ambassador of God who frequently visits earth to meet God's creations; he takes their grievances, requests and desires to the court of Lord Vishnu, one of the Gods in the holy trinity. When things got too difficult or uncontrollable on earth, Lord Vishnu himself would take birth on the planet as an avatar to set things right. But in periods of normalcy, his messenger, Narad Muni, was enough to ensure order.

As he prayed to top the school, Gulveer's face would appear time and again in his mind. After he had finished with his prayers and had made his request politely, Manikchand did not wait for Gulveer at the junction as he usually did. Instead, he continued on his way to school by himself. Once he reached school, he would be lost in his thoughts and did not interact much with anybody, not even Gulveer. Soon, this became a habit. Every day, he would stop at the temple, pray to the deity and then remain aloof from everyone at school for the rest of the day.

One day, all of a sudden, Gulveer stopped coming to school. At that time, it didn't affect Manikchand. He was still engrossed in a world of his own which mainly revolved around his studies. Manikchand wrote the exams and was happy with his efforts. Not only that, his dreams had come true. He had topped the school.

Meanwhile, once the results had been declared, he learnt that Gulveer had riddled with the effects of smallpox, which was why he could not write the exams. Manikchand knew how dreaded a disease smallpox was, and how it killed children in hordes. Those who survived had their faces and bodies scarred with ugly blotches.

Manikchand was suddenly overcome by impenetrable guilt. He felt he had betrayed his best friend and had denied him his rightful place. He was tormented by remorse and was unable to concentrate on anything. To Hirachand's dismay, Manikchand refused to study any further. He also took a vow to never go to a temple and declared that he would never pray for anything for the rest of his life. However, Manikchand could not muster up the courage to meet Gulveer or to enquire about his well-being. The guilt was overwhelming and he was also angered by his indifference and blind ambition. He didn't know how he would manage it if he had to face his erstwhile best friend.

Manikchand lived a rudderless life for many years. In order to calm himself and rid himself of the guilt, anger and anxiety that tormented him, he started wrestling. He fought ruthlessly and often won tournaments against stronger adversaries. Manikchand would fight to the finish, but many times, even fainted in the ring. To everyone else, it seemed as if he was punishing himself for what he perceived as his sin.

To pacify him and get him settled in life, Hirachand got Manikchand married. He also persuaded him to join the family business. Manikchand would half-heartedly come to the shop and would, on most occasions, sit there, looking distracted and lost. The only person in whom he confided occasionally was his wife, Rukmani. His life plodded along, defined by dull routine with no silver lining outlining his dark clouds. Unfortunately for him, he and his wife could not conceive a child. Life for Manikchand turned out to be perpetual drudgery. The only time he would perk up and look happy was in the presence of Ramveer, his old friend, who had been a year senior to him in school.

Ramveer had joined the British army as a sepoy soon after

leaving school. He visited Hisar once a year for two months, during his annual leave. During those months, Manikchand and he would spend time together almost every evening. Ramveer would narrate tales of his long rail journeys to take part in various wars and quell armed-resistance in different parts of British-occupied India. He would bring with him bottles of rum, supplied by the army canteen and they would chat and laugh all evening over a few drinks. Ramveer would tell Manikchand about life in the cantonments and the way the British officers walked with their ladies, hand-in-hand, often kissing in public. He told him about how the English women were averse to breastfeeding, and instead employed wet nurses so that they themselves could eternally stay young and pretty. Ramveer occasionally took Manikchand to Delhi to enjoy a mehfil: a night of song and poetry, with sensuous nautch girls swaying to the soulful music. Ramveer opened up a whole new world to Manikchand, bringing cheer and light to his otherwise lacklustre existence. They would fondly cradle memories about their school days, their classmates and teachers.

One day, Manikchand plucked up the courage and asked about Gulveer Chaudhary. Everybody seemed to have forgotten him. Manikchand had finally gained the resolve to open up a closed and painful chapter of his life, and he would see it through.

Manikchand, along with Ramveer, went to Gulveer's village to check on him. There, they found out that the smallpox had almost killed Gulveer and it had taken him many months to recover. After that, he wandered aimlessly for many years, finally joining an extremist group committed to gaining independence from the British through violent means, and fled the village. Beyond that, the local kotwali had little information about him.

Years later, on one of his trips to that very village, Ramveer brought news of Gulveer. A few local sources had told him that Gulveer had escaped to the Himalayas and had become a saint—a Naga sadhu who wandered around almost naked, with no worldly possessions. It was considered the most difficult path to salvation, and only a very few were capable of living such a life of detachment, hatha yoga, *tapasya* and complete renunciation. Gulveer was now known as Chaudhary Baba, the name given to him by his followers. Apparently, he lived in Gangotri, the source of the holy Ganga.

The next spring, Manikchand decided to make the long and difficult journey into the Himalayas in search of Chaudhary Baba. People usually undertook such difficult pilgrimages only after completing the *grahast* phase, and on entering *vanaprasta*. For Manikchand, however, it was not a pilgrimage, but a quest.

There were no motorable roads after Rishikesh, and he had to walk on foot for days together. He would sleep in small temples on the way, walking along the banks of the river Ganges to reach her source. After Karnaprayag, the journey became extremely tough. Manikchand had to cross the fiercely flowing river over make shift log bridges laid by the villagers. On the last stretch, he had to walk through thick forests, crawling along with wild creatures. Ultimately, the tall trees, the pines, the bushes and the ferns were all left behind, and the mountains became rocky, snow-covered and bare. It was a beautiful rugged place, pristine, with no human habitation. This was where Chaudhary Baba lived.

Manikchand found him living in a small hut close to the stream. He was unkempt and bearded but had the youthfulness and vigour of the Gulveer that Manikchand remembered. When Manikchand stumbled into the hut, no introductions were needed; the mystic seemed to already know Manikchand's past,

present and future. It was as if their souls were connected through many cycles of birth and death. The Baba welcomed him silently, not uttering a single word. Manikchand smiled at him, then collected himself and bowed with a namaste. No words were exchanged.

Manikchand spent many days with the mystic and was soon immersed in the routine of *maun, dhyana, sadhna* and *tapasya*. Finally, after many days, the mystic spoke to him. 'You are destined to be rich and famous. You will reach a pedestal that nobody in your town has ever attained. You will be blessed with an obedient and worthy son who will make you proud.'

After spending many days and months in the Himalayas, Manikchand had started looking like a saint himself. He decided to return to Hisar. So, he undertook the difficult journey back to the plains. When he finally reached Hisar, he had been completely transformed by his encounter with the Baba.

Soon Manikchand asked Rukmani to accompany him to Delhi. They went to Delhi in a government-run bus. From the bus stand, they took a cycle rickshaw to the newly built, Lady Hardinge Hospital, which exclusively accommodated women in British India's new capital. An Irish gynaecologist examined Rukmani and informed her that her ovaries were normal; however, there was a blockage in the ovarian tube that was preventing the movement of the ova to the fallopian tube, leading to a condition where she could not conceive. Nevertheless, her disorder was treatable, only that the treatment would require many more visits to Delhi. Rukmani was now in her late thirties. Many of her peers had already become grandmothers. She had lost all hope of giving birth to a child. Although her desire for motherhood had not wavered an inch, she was sceptical. It was difficult to explain their secret visits to Delhi to the rest of the family. They had no relatives in the city. They couldn't provide an excuse; Manikchand was known for being non-religious since he never visited any temples. Anyway, fortunately for them, the family came to terms with their frequent, unannounced journeys. They joked that it was probably the last spark of romance for the ageing couple. They assumed the couple perhaps went to watch a movie or two in one of Delhi's theatres or went to the city's markets, renowned for their delicious eateries. Nobody knew what exactly they were doing in Delhi, but everyone was quite surprised when they received the news that Rukmani was pregnant. That set many tongues wagging.

A son was born to Rukmani and Manikchand on a cold wintry night. The couple were overjoyed with their blessing. For Manikchand, life suddenly seemed worthwhile and meaningful.

Now that the visits to Delhi had ended and Manikchand had attained fatherhood, something he had long craved for, he began to concentrate on the business.

The war clouds were filling the skies and soon British India was fighting alongside the allied forces in the war against Hitler. Manikchand had been watching the movements of commodities in the markets for many years. He knew that metal prices were bound to rise as huge quantities of metal would be needed to cater to the war machine. Manikchand started procuring and hoarding metals.

The search for metals took Manikchand across the length and breadth of the Indian subcontinent. The Indian economy had moved along with the network of railway lines that connected its capital to other provinces and territories, creating a web of rail routes around mines, ports, agricultural markets, metropolises and military establishments. India was administered through this network, in addition to the communication infrastructure provided by post offices and radio stations.

Manikchand travelled by rail to the great cities of Lahore, Rawalpindi and Peshawar in the north-west, to Calcutta, Dhaka, Guwahati and Rangoon in the east. He travelled to Madras and Cochin in the south and to Varanasi, Delhi and Shimla in the north. Sometimes, he had to go further, beyond the railheads, travelling in bullock carts and on foot to procure metal. The railways snaked through thick forests, deep crevices, uninhabited landscapes, rivers, mountains, plateaus and deserts. It ferried metals, minerals, timber, troops, weapons, pilgrims and passengers across the subcontinent. Manikchand followed its path.

To begin with, Manikchand travelled in third class, mingling with the mango people, fakirs, storytellers and thugs. He had sold his house to start his fledgling business, and they had all moved to a rented place. Rukmani was worried and anxious because he had sold all her jewellery in his haste to buy metal. Once he began trading, the money started to circulate and return back to the household. There were significant profits to be made in trading metals during the war time. As his economic stature improved, Manikchand frequented the safer and more comfortable second class. Subsequently, once he became richer, he upgraded to first-class travel. This gave him the opportunity to mingle with European landlords, big businessmen, high-ranking officers and the other elite. He found himself in a new world, with a new culture and etiquette, one that was strange yet fascinating. Manikchand slowly became confident about conversing in English, dining with a fork and knife, wearing tailored suits and reading English newspapers. In his haste to collect and hoard iron, aluminium, copper and other metals from the cheapest sources, Manikchand was spending more and more time travelling by rail. On the journeys, he would often be invited to travel as a guest of some royal family, who regularly travelled in their own saloons with private bedrooms, a dining area, bar, cloakrooms, pantry and servants' compartment.

Once Britain entered the war, metal prices skyrocketed. British India was given a target to enrol men and assemble arms, ammunition, weapons and supplies for the military. Ordnance factories were set up all over the country. Manikchand's metal inventory was in great demand. He became very rich; very quickly. On a request from the District Collector, he once donated a significant quantity of metal to the government, which fetched him a title. He was now a Rai Bahadur of the British government. Now, Manikchand was not only rich, but also a powerful and famous man in the region. He not only repurchased what he had sold to arrange for funds, but also built a massive, opulent mansion to match his changed lifestyle.

Now that he had a son, a successful business, wealth and repute, Manikchand paid a visit to Chaudhary Baba, along with Rukmani and his son, Lakshmichand. A single lane road had been laid now, and it went right up to Gangotri. However, on reaching the source of the river, they discovered that the mystic was no longer there. He had moved to Gaumukh, the place where the holy Ganges emerges as a small stream. Rukmani was already tired from the long, arduous journey and decided to stay back in Gangotri. Manikchand and Lakshmichand, along with a few porters, continued their journey.

Chaudhary Baba lived in a hut, not far from Gaumukh.

Manikchand told him how he had been blessed with a son. He also narrated the saga of his journey to wealth. He thanked the saint for his blessings. The mystic gave him an inscrutable smile and told Manikchand, 'Lakshmi, the Goddess of Wealth, is always travelling; she likes to wander rather than sit tight.' He was very happy to see Manikchand's child. He placed his hand on Lakshmichand's head and prophesied, 'Your son will outperform you and will do very well in life.'

Manikchand was very happy on hearing the saint's prediction for his son's future. However, the earlier utterance of the mystic puzzled him. If Lakshmi was mobile, was it not possible that she could eventually move away from him? Was there any way to change this particular trait of the Goddess of Wealth? Was there any method by which wealth could remain with him and his family forever? He conveyed his questions to the Baba.

The saint remained silent. After a few days of deep pondering, the saint again spoke. 'You need to keep circulating wealth. Never try to bind the Goddess of Wealth, secure it tightly or imprison her. If you do, wealth will leave you with the same vigour as it came.'

'But there are principles involved in the circulation of money,' said Manikchand thoughtfully. 'You can't do that thoughtlessly, in an unplanned and random way.'

'The only other way is to receive the blessings of Saraswati, the Goddess of Knowledge, who is Goddess Lakshmi's younger sister,' said the mystic. 'Once you have Saraswati, Lakshmi may stay longer, as she likes her sister's company.'

Manikchand was content with the mystic's reply; he felt he was better armed and prepared for the future. By the time he returned to Gangotri, he had already changed his son's name.

Now, the world would know him as Saraswatichand. When the family returned to Hisar, he looked for a resident British teacher to teach his son the English language. Over time, he hired many more teachers to teach young Saraswatichand mathematics and science. He also set up a library for his son in the mansion, with the vast array of books he imported from England. He was not going to scrounge on giving his son the best of education and knowledge.

Manikchand rented a house in Delhi where Rukmani and Saraswati could live, making sure that Saraswati could study in the best English medium school, run by missionaries. Saraswati was a bright child, quick to learn and hungry for knowledge. However, his mother doted on him and spoilt him often, distracting him from his studies. Thus, when it was time for Saraswati to go to college, Manikchand decided to send him far off to South India, to study engineering. He knew Madras would provide him with the best environment to learn and shape a bright future, away from the all-encompassing protection of his parents. Guindy College of Engineering was one of the most sought-after places to study engineering, and the most accomplished of students from all over the country vied to be admitted to this esteemed institution. Once Saraswatichand completed engineering from Guindy, the obvious way forward was to go abroad for higher studies. Manikchand left no stone unturned to please the Goddess of Knowledge, Saraswati, in order to cajole and ensure a longer abode for her sister Lakshmi, the Goddess of Wealth.

Manikchand was proud of his son. Saraswatichand was intelligent, tall and handsome. He had always excelled in academics. Now he was an alumnus of one of the best business schools of the world: Wharton, in the United States, which had emerged as a superpower in the new world order. In addition to learning the curriculum, the business school gave him exposure to the rest of the world, taught him etiquette, helped him build a formidable network and gave him the confidence to think big. All his classmates had very similar dreams. Initially, most of them wanted to undergo training in leading international firms and later become entrepreneurs and business leaders.

Manikchand took Saraswati to meet Chaudhary Baba once he had graduated from business school. After a long, tedious drive along the serpentine mountain road to Gangotri, the father and son duo trekked on a narrow pathway to Gaumukh to reach the tiny cottage in which Chaudhary Baba now resided.

Baba was happy to see Saraswati and gave him his blessings. Manikchand proudly told the mystic about Saraswati's various achievements. Baba listened enthusiastically to Manikchand's gushing praise of his son. A shy Saraswati sat with a sheepish smile on his face, awkward at being eulogised about in such a lavish manner. He was not used to being showered with so much praise by his father.

Saraswati told the saint of his plan to work in a multinational company to gain experience; he also wanted to figure out what he would really like to do. He said that he eventually wanted to get into manufacturing and put to use his engineering education. The mystic appeared enthusiastic as he once again blessed Saraswati. 'You will do very well in life and be very successful in all your endeavours. Life is unpredictable, so do not ponder too much. Do what you like and do it quickly. You never know how much time you have,' said the mystic. On hearing this, Manikchand turned pale. He knew that the mystic was not mincing his words and that what he had just heard would have serious consequences in their future.

The saint was making an ominous forecast and Manikchand would have to take corrective actions, on a war footing. His son, Saraswati, needed to do something momentous and, for that to happen, time would be a major constraint. Manikchand immediately started looking for a partner for Saraswati—someone who was beautiful, educated and from a good family. But beyond and above all these attributes, her horoscope needed to support that of Saraswati's. She could not have an astral combination for widowhood. That would bless Saraswati with a longer life.

In just a few weeks, Usha, a slim, beautiful, convent-educated and well-mannered girl from an affluent family in Delhi was found to be a suitable match. Her father exported spices and had made a fortune in the business. Usha's horoscope matched Saraswati's; the presence of the exalted Jupiter in her seventh house indicated a famous and rich husband. It also bestowed her with good character and pleasant manners.

Manikchand then asked Saraswati to relinquish all his other plans behind and start a business. There were fewer opportunities in India; it was a protected, inward-looking economy, shackled by an all-pervasive licence raj. Saraswati felt it was not conducive to growth. Corruption had become a way of life and it was difficult to establish anything worthwhile, without proper patronage. Saraswati was not cut out to deal with the red-tape and to conduct a business in such an environment.

After prolonged deliberations, Manikchand provided him with enough funds to explore business environments in other countries. The business school network helped Saraswati get a loan to acquire a closed foundry in Eastern Europe.

Saraswati and Usha travelled together to set up home in

Europe. They moved from one country to another, and ultimately, settled in Berlin in West Germany. The country provided them with a good life, a highly skilled and disciplined workforce and ample scope to expand their business—not only in Germany, but all over Europe as well.

Germany soon became their home, with both of them fluent in its many dialects. Usha was a homemaker and steadfastly stood by her husband. She was religious, homely and devoted to him. Saraswati and Usha gave birth to a girl after a few years of marriage. As their business grew, the couple, along with their daughter, Neha, rented a large house in an upmarket locality. Saraswati's business house was now flourishing and he had named it Saraswati Steel. The company had set up its headquarters in Berlin, with steel mills and foundries established in various corners of several countries.

Ruzbeh, his classmate from business school, joined Saraswati Steel and infused some share capital into the company. Ruzbeh was a down-to-earth man. He loved walking around project sites: supervising the remodelling of old foundries and setting up rolling mills from scratch, managing people and building teams. His commitment and hard work would enthuse them all. The European engineers and field workers were devoted to the company and their work, but they needed a compassionate boss—one who heard them out, was ready to get his hands dirty, treat them as equals and guide them well. Ruzbeh turned out to be the right man for the job. On one hand, he was humble, but on the other, persuasive, keeping an eye on everything while monitoring independent, individual tasks. Ruzbeh's sharp acumen, support and devotion to work propelled Saraswati Steel to become one of the leading steel manufacturers in Europe.

After Saraswati left to set up life in Europe, Manikchand began to feel extremely lonely. He had never felt alone when Saraswati had gone abroad to study. Back then, he'd felt that it was temporary, that his son would come back and take over the reins of his business. But his son was gone and, to make matters worse, Manik was stuck where he was. He felt helpless because he was unable to leave everything and move to be with his son. Rukmani's health was failing, so there was no question of moving to another country. Rukmani silently but firmly believed that Manikchand was responsible for her loneliness. She felt that it was because of him that her precious son had to leave. If Manikchand had not put these ideas into her son's head and had not kept urging him to find success quickly, he would have remained next to his parents. The couple continued to live in the mammoth mansion; but it was like a huge old tree whose branches and leaves had been chopped off, leaving only the gnarled trunk and the roots.

Saraswati would visit them at least once a year, along with Usha and Neha. These visits would be hectic and short. Usha also looked forward to spending a few days, of their short visit, with her parents and siblings. Relatives and friends would come in hordes to see the visitors who lived abroad, ogling at them with great admiration.

Even before they knew it, the children would start to pack and would all be gone, leaving Manikchand and Rukmani alone for months together. Even after Rukmani's death, Manikchand could not gather the courage and confidence to leave Hisar. He was too deeply rooted here and it felt impossible to move. Everything in Hisar was familiar to him and, at this ripe old age, he wasn't keen on uprooting himself, leaving everything that he was attached to, and move to live in an alien land. Deep down in his heart, Manikchand had this fervent desire that one day Saraswati and his family would come back to where they all belonged.

During one of his visits, Manikchand decided to take Saraswati once again to meet Chaudhary Baba. The father and son duo made the long gruelling journey to the Himalayas. Manikchand was old and quite frail by now. In spite of his strong will, his ageing body could not make it to the abode of Chaudhary Baba, so Manikchand had to culminate the journey at a temple on the banks of the river.

From here, Saraswati had to make the journey alone. It took him days to reach the seer, who had moved even further, to a more inaccessible and isolated site.

The saint was as welcoming as ever; he made Saraswati feel comfortable in his small hut. Saraswati stayed in the remote hut for several days. He had nothing to ask the Baba for himself. Now his concern was Neha. Baba looked towards the shining stars, glittering like diamonds in the inky black sky, and said, 'From here, your ride will be on the chariot of wealth. Neha will be much more successful than you. She will lead the world and will provide hope and relief to mankind. She will be a saviour.' Saraswati was rather puzzled by this prophesy.

'In today's world, one has to wield enormous power to make a difference. Neha will be a queen, continued the mystic. 'The Rajyogas are of many kinds. Being rich, famous and powerful are three hierarchical orders of the Rajyogas. But above all this, there is a superior Rajyoga and that is bestowed only to the saints.'

Saraswati was dumbstruck. This was not what he had envisioned for his only daughter. Neha was not going to be a saint, he decided. He would much rather prefer that she remain a queen; Saraswati was determined that he would do whatever it took to ensure this. Saraswati dreamt of a comfortable, sheltered life for Neha, free from the vagaries of the world. He would provide her with luxury and gift her the best education. Before he left Chaudhary Baba's austere hut, he announced, 'Neha will have nothing to do with sainthood. She is too fragile to live such a harsh life.' He would keep her sheltered from the pains and quirks of the real world. Saraswati will make all efforts to get her married in an affluent family and keep her away from all influence of austerity and sainthood. Neha would be groomed to be a queen, he resolved.

Saraswati did not mention anything about his conversation with the Baba to Manikchand. They undertook their tedious journey back to Hisar mostly in silence. After a few days, Saraswati took leave of his father and went back to Berlin. From then on, his visits to India became less frequent. Even when he did come, he preferred to travel alone on those rare occasions, leaving Usha and Neha behind in Germany.

Now that his wife was no more, Manik was being looked after by his nephews and a battery of loyal servants, who had been a part of the household for decades. Lately, Saraswati had been receiving news about Manikchand's deteriorating health. Manikchand was mostly bedridden now, and he had hardly left the house for months together. Repeated requests that he join them in Europe for better health care had fallen on deaf ears. Manikchand was very particular that he spent his remaining days in the city of his ancestors; he would breathe his last where his father, his grandfather and his great grandfather had lived and died.

Saraswati, Usha and little Neha arrived at Delhi airport on a

warm morning after a six-hour flight from the Frankfurt Airport. During the entire journey, Saraswati barely spoke and hardly ate anything. He was lost in his own thoughts, as if preparing himself for the agony that lay waiting ahead.

Unlike their earlier journeys, they were travelling light, with no check-in baggage. They were not carrying suitcases overflowing with foreign goods to gift relatives. He did not go to the duty-free area to buy cigarettes, liquor, chocolates and perfumes, something he had always done on all his earlier journeys back to India. At Frankfurt Airport, Saraswati confined himself to the airport lounge, waiting eagerly for the departure to be announced, while his wife kept the baby engaged.

The New Delhi airport was even worse than it had been earlier. The structure had deteriorated, and there were leaking taps, stinking toilets, negligent emigration staff, utter chaos at customs, yelling taxi drivers, tired policemen and notorious touts trying to fleece people in broad daylight. His first cousin, Ratan, had come to pick them up. Their luggage was put on the carrier over the roof of the car and tied down with a rope since the boot was already occupied with items being ferried by the driver.

During the journey, Ratan updated Saraswati about Manik's worsening condition. This upset Saraswati even more; he appeared extremely disturbed. Ratan tried to initiate some polite conversation but he only received curt, monosyllabic replies thereafter. Soon, Ratan lost his patience and, ignoring the guests, began to chat with the driver about mundane things all the way to the house.

The ride within the city was smooth, traffic was sparse and the city of babus was fast asleep on a Sunday morning. Darkness once again started enveloping the landscape as they approached

Sonepat. The bright sunlit morning was engulfed by dark clouds as the weather rapidly changed. A sandstorm was approaching and visibility on the road was low. The trucks and buses had started to park along roadside dhabas, deciding to wait until the sandstorm had passed.

The wind was strong, swooping down and around buildings, howling eerily. They had to roll up the windows of their non-air-conditioned Ambassador car to keep the dust from entering. The driver had to get down twice to secure their luggage by tightening the cords.

As they drove, they could see the carcass of a big animal at a distance, probably a dead buffalo. It was lying on its side in the middle of the road. A group of vultures had surrounded it and they were tearing the flesh out of the dead animal with their strong beaks. Many more were sitting hunched on a tree, waiting for their turn. Saraswati and Usha were used to the sight of these large, ugly, fierce birds eating dead cows, cattle and dogs. But for Neha, it was a revolting sight. She had never seen anything like this before, something so brutal and primeval. She flinched in fear, shivering and crying.

The sandstorm worsened and soon, nothing was visible. They had to stop the car and park on the side of the road because of a complete lack of visibility. Suddenly, lightning flashed, followed by the loud rumble of thunder. Ratan advised them to get out of the car and take shelter in a small brick layered roadside shop.

The vultures were not far from where they rested. Neha could see them flying away from the prey, having already feasted on the carcass, fluttering over them at an arm's distance as they left the car. It was the scariest sight she had ever experienced in her young life. The whirling, wailing wind, the thud and crash of falling trees,

the roar of thunder, the flashes of lightning streaking across the sky, the blinding dust, the surreal darkness and the flapping of the menacing vultures over their heads, as they hurriedly moved into the shelter, left her shaking.

Soon, the sandstorm subsided, the thunder stopped and a light drizzle and golden sunshine bathed the landscape once again. They secured their luggage, got back in the car and set off.

The vultures, once again, closed in, their wings beating a terrifying rhythm above their heads as they returned to their prey to pick the carcass, clean to the bone.

The rest of the journey was smooth. Neha had been so scared and traumatised that she had buried her head in her mother's belly. She did not raise her head or open her eyes until they reached the portico of their large ancestral mansion. By the time they reached, Manik's soul had already departed from his body after a forlorn and unending wait for his son.

3

Sridhar—The Solitary Seeker

Sridhar was born in the remote temple town of Vaitheeswaran Koil, near Kumbakonam in the State of Madras. Vaitheeswaran Koil is a small, sleepy town in the Cauvery Delta, the rice bowl of South India. Its name and existence is derived from the eponymous big temple there, devoted to the red planet, Mars. A large *Agraharam*, where the Brahmin community lives, encircles the temple. This area was dotted with *vedashalas*, granaries, quarters for the *devadasis* and teachers of Carnatic music and classical dance. Several fortune tellers of varrying repute, adept in the craft of prediction called *nadijyothisham*, had set up shop in the lanes and by-lanes around the temple. Most of the land in this area belonged to the Lord, and the peasants willingly offered a part of their produce to the main deity, Shiva; the God of Destruction.

The delta area of Tamil Nadu had been ruled by the Chola kings for centuries. The Cholas built large magnificent temples, devoted to stars, planets and other celestial nodes of the solar system. In the geo-centric astronomy of ancient India, the Sun and the Moon had the status of planets, right alongside Mars, Mercury, Saturn, Jupiter and Venus. As per the Hindu belief, these planets, along with the two nodes, namely Rahu and Ketu—both, created destiny as well as also destroyed it. They bestowed luck, happiness and prosperity. The very same planets, depending on their position and other aspects, could also cause sorrows, disasters and deaths.

Most of the temples the Cholas had built were colossal and grand affairs, devoted to the planets of destiny. In all these temples, the chief deity was Shiva. The planets, to appease whom the pilgrims predominantly came from all over the subcontinent, were only given a place in the outer circle, while Lord Shiva reigned supreme within the sanctum sanctorum.

The Cholas had also built large ships and were great traders. They had a strong military and with their naval power and merchant ships, the stamp of their influence spread across the whole of Southeast Asia. They not only spread their culture, but built magnificent temples devoted to Hindu Gods and Goddesses.

During the British rule, ship building by the Indians was made a criminal offence, and thus, this great industry was lost to the country. In the latter half of the eighteenth century, Veerapandiya Kattabomman defied law and built a ship, in which he later sailed the Indian Ocean. His venture was registered as an offence and for this, he was tried in a court of law and hurriedly hanged. This made him a martyr and daredevil freedom fighter often depicted as a symbol of national pride, symbolised in the floats exhibited in the Republic Day parade at New Delhi; the capital of the Indian Republic.

Sridhar lived in a large joint family. Hailing from a Brahmin family, his grandfather, his father and his uncles were all part of a clan that managed the temple; they lived in the agraharam next to it. His mother was from Sirkazhi, where her family managed the other big temple. His aunts and sisters were married into various families all along the Cauvery Delta, managing the Navagraha and other Shaivite temples.

The Shaivite Iyer Brahmins married amongst themselves, lived in *agraharams* and were taught to manage the temples of Lord Shiva and his avatars. In addition to keeping their distance from other castes and communities, they were also averse to being in the company of Iyengar Brahmins, who were worshippers of Lord Vishnu and belonged to the Vaishnavite sect. At one point of time, the antagonism between these two sects grew so deep that Hinduism almost split into two separate religions. The religious leaders of the communities had to intervene and bring them together by introducing the cult of God, Ayappan, born out of intimacy between Shiva and Vishnu—both males. But one of them had taken the form of a woman in this blessed union. Now, both the cults were obliged to pray to Ayappan, the offspring of their revered deities, Shiva and Vishnu. Thus, a major cleaving of Hinduism, one of the most ancient religions in the world, was prevented.

Sridhar was destined to be a priest. He learnt the patterns of the ancient art of astrology from his elders. He learnt about the Brahmin rituals to appease the Gods, and their different avatars during different seasons and during different parts of the day. He learnt about the food, flowers and clothes liked by different deities. He learnt the chants, hymns and music to please the deities. He learnt the traditional methods to awaken the deities in the early hours of the day and the methods to finally enable them to attain their sleep at night. He learnt about special prayers for special occasions.

Sridhar was taught the nature and characteristics of the signs of the zodiac, the rashis and the nakshatras. He learnt the interplay of the zodiac signs, their lords and the planets occupying each sign. He understood the finer aspects of celestial movements and their impact on worldly beings. Sridhar learnt the mathematics behind preparing a horoscope and the methods to calculate the periods and sub-periods of one's life. He was taught the system of matching horoscopes for partnership, friendship and marriage. He could calculate and advise people on the most auspicious time, for wedding ceremonies, lighting the funeral fire, starting important journeys and all other significant decisions.

The priests at Vaitheeswaran Koil were known for a specialised system of astrology called *nadijyothisham*, which claims to have a palm leaf preserved for every human being who has lived on earth and also for those destined to be born in the future. These palm leaves, interpreted by priests with specialised knowledge, could tell people about their past, present, future and even about their lives lived in earlier births..

Soon after Independence, the management of the temples was taken over by the government and the priests became paid employees. Very soon, it became difficult for them to sustain their large families on the meagre salaries they received. It was the end of life as they had known it—a life steeped in tradition and rituals, where daily living revolved around the temple and worship and other esoteric practices. It was time for them to move on from this cocooned existence.

Sridhar pursued his schooling in the adjoining town of Mayiladuthurai, and widened his horizons by going to the temple town of Thanjavur to pursue higher studies in college. Thereafter, he qualified for admission in Guindy College of Engineering in Madras. The college was one of the finest established in British India. Its counterpart in Roorkee, in the foothills of the Himalayas, advanced to become an Indian Institute of Technology (IIT), which is considered a formidable brand of higher education in India—an institution of excellence. The Guindy Institute could never get this tag as an IIT already existed on the other side of the road. However, in terms of staff training and eminence, it matched the very best of the best engineering institutes in the country. Sridhar studied civil engineering, which was the most sought-after branch in the college.

His roommate in the hostel was a young lad from North India who was trying to navigate life in one of the most traditional South Indian cities. Sridhar could see that it was a cultural shock for the lad. Saraswatichand had no knowledge of Tamil and had a great longing for wheat, the staple cereal beyond the Vindhyas, something that was hardly cooked or consumed in Madras. Otherwise, he was a pleasant and sensible person who quickly adapted to this new environment. It did not take much time for Sridhar and the North Indian boy to become good friends.

In spite of the wide cultural chasm between them, they had many similarities between them. They were both vegetarians, had a sweet tooth and were new to the metropolis; both were sincere, hardworking and God-fearing. Their horoscopes seemed to have matched well, and they became very close buddies.

Sridhar had led an insulated existence in a small village, steeped in tradition. He had never been taught to think for himself; instead, he was taught to listen, to learn, to abide by blind faith. He was used to being led: led by his elders in practising various rituals, led by his father, led by his teachers and above

all, led by his horoscope.

The knowledge of astrology, the predisposition of one's life in a nadi leaf, the strong and enduring impact of the big temple, the practice of starting a day after analysing the movement of stars and judging the muhurtam had a huge impact on his free will and ability to take decisions.

For him, life was circumscribed by fate, stars, time and rituals. He looked at life through his horoscope. His birth chart was his biggest liability, his biggest shackle; hindering him, cautioning him and limiting him all the time. He could not make friends, take risks or be outgoing, unless the stars permitted it. This knowledge chained him to his destiny, largely crushing his free will.

The grandeur of civil engineering, the mega structures, the mega-planners, the builders of the tallest skyscrapers, longest bridges, highways, tunnels and reclamations were all products of free will. If these pioneers had been similarly circumscribed and trapped within their horoscopes, such imagination, such feats, such marvels would have never been possible. Yet, there was something in him which kept him tied to the zodiac and the planets within them. His past and his ancestry always kept him trapped within these archetypes, thereby stalling his dreams.

Sridhar and Saraswati had a unique bond, blessed by the stars. Saraswati was an extrovert, and one who was in a hurry to achieve. He was willing to take bold risks to see his ideas take fruition. His ideals and his actions were synchronised. He wasted neither time nor effort on things that were not within the horizon of his ambitions. For him, everything else was sheer essentialities, entertainment or 'time pass'. He was an obsessive doer.

Sridhar, on the other hand, was inhibited, inward-looking and cautious. He thought too much and analysed much, and took limited or no concrete action. Hailing from a small village where service to God was the mantra, he was naive about metropolitan living and reluctant to embrace change. His life was trapped in his horoscope which he naively but spontaneously kept referring to whenever he had to initiate anything significant.

In order to begin anything and everything, his planets, their orientation and their dynamic location and interactions came unconsciously to his mind. And he would discover that something was lacking or out of place, thus forcing him to postpone his actions. Sridhar was so obsessed and so handicapped that opportunities kept flying past him, and he could never grab them, steeped as he was in indecision and superstition.

For Saraswati, Sridhar was a healer. Whenever Saraswati's actions failed, he would be in a state of turmoil, Sridhar would come to his rescue, swiftly creating a celestial design for such failures. He would encourage Saraswati to work harder, to get back on his feet and make yet another attempt. The same stars that restricted and bound Sridhar's life provided dynamism and a never-say-die approach for Saraswati.

After completing his bachelor's degree in engineering, Sridhar completed his Masters, and then enrolled as a junior faculty member at the college in Guindy. Saraswati, on the other hand, broadened his horizons. He took his graduate record examination and got himself enrolled in a leading business school at Wharton, Pennsylvania in the United States.

Although they were now in two different continents, they kept in touch. The odd letter every month or two, or an exorbitantly priced international call, kept the umbilical cord intact. Sridhar

would write to Saraswati of the strides in research and development in the field of engineering. Sridhar was Saraswati's sole link to engineering and academia and to many of their classmates, who had now moved to various parts of the country and the world in pursuance of their careers. The ever-expanding public sector was their first choice. A few had joined the private sector or had migrated to other fields and businesses. And a miniscule few, like Sridhar, had stayed put in their alma mater.

Saraswati had invited him to Germany when he first took over the old foundry, and Sridhar had accepted the invitation. Saraswati had also invited him for his wedding at Hisar, to which Sridhar had joyously gone and had stood beside him, like the brother Saraswati never had.

The presence of the enemy lord and a fierce planet in the seventh house of marriage had done away with any desire for marriage—or even a partnership—as far as Sridhar was concerned. It never occurred to him to challenge his destiny, which was confined in a maze of celestial movements, on a prescription written on a *nadi* leaf, preserved for times immemorial and written in an ancient language which only a few could decipher. He didn't have the courage to fight what the stars had destined for him. He found comfort and security in following them instead.

Yes, life was lonely and constrained, but it was at least risk-averse and safe, guided by the knowledge of a so-called science, a science which still considered the sun to be a planet revolving around the earth. To him, it still made sense, and it often worked.

When Saraswati made him an offer to join him in a nascent business that needed the undertaking of major civil works and maintenance, he relented and put aside his horoscope. It was his first step out of the cocoon into something unknown. Initially, he joined Saraswati at Berlin without severing his lien from his permanent teaching job. It was only later that he became a full-time employee.

Sridhar was happy drawing a fixed salary as an employee, and he never acquired even a single share of the company, fearing the wrath of the planets. But over time, Sridhar became the biggest asset of Saraswati Steel. He and Saraswati had built it from scratch to become a global enterprise, one as a leader and the other as Saraswati's most trusted adviser, friend and guide.

4

Brigette—The Sculptor of Destiny

Brigette had a rickety childhood. Her unwed mother left her to become a nun and devote her life to the Lord; Brigette was nursed and groomed by her grandmother, far within a remote village in the Black Forest. Her mother never returned. Her grandmother adopted her and sheltered her, but could not provide her with a worthy childhood. Her co-born in the village, her cousins, her relatives were all poor. She was always the one to be offered the last piece of the birthday cake, last to be invited for Christmas gatherings and the last to be handed over a gift. She always wore darned dresses her cousins had outgrown, shoes that no one desired; she carried discarded school bags and read from outlived books. But she studied, and thought of her education as the sole way out of her humiliating and worthless life, the only ticket to escape her troubled existence. It was from books she learnt that a 'bastard' is a child born out of wedlock, and from books that she realised how she was ship-wrecked from infancy. And yet, books were her solace and her hope.

She created a friendship with numbers and soon become a mathematics champion.

Numbers don't disguise themselves. They don't lie. They are not manipulative. Numbers are the real truth. They are not partial.

She started to master numbers: algebra, geometry, trigonometry, algorithm, matrix and integrations. Her mastery of numbers brought her the attention she wanted. She topped all the mathematical quizzes and became the undisputed rank holder. Her brilliance in mathematics made science easy for her. She topped in every subject, other than German and social sciences. She could never develop any real liking for words or emotions, they were just stories of heroism or romance and fairy tales.

For her, they were empty and worthless narratives with no numeric strength. They were partial, and all they did was provide a space for the haves and the have-nots, for the rich and the poor, for the orators and the audience, for the word crafters and the innocents, for the preacher and the preached, for the oppressor and the oppressed, for the kings and their subjects; they formed the divide between her and her cousins. Humanities reminded her of her mother who abandoned her, whose love she was never bestowed with. It brought her to an old, frail and helpless grandmother, and to her fathomless pain. She wanted to escape to ensure that she would not have a child who would have to face this trauma. She wanted to create a future with no semblance to her past and she could do so with numbers.

Numbers gave her hope and opportunity. The school headmaster recommended her name for the school of accountancy in Berlin. Her romance with numbers soon made her the best student in the school of accountancy.

She never returned to her village. Not even to see her ailing

old grandmother. Instead, Brigette wanted to create a new world and bring her grandmother to that world, her world. During vacations, she would take odd jobs and earn enough to get through the academic year.

The company laws made accountancy a selling branch of education. There was no dearth of assignments and high-salaried jobs. The stock market boom made account consultants highly prized, and it was a lucrative profession. Everything looked rosy and nice.

Then one day, Brigette fell in love, naively and foolishly. Rio was one of the first to see the girl in her, who longed to laugh and longed to be loved. He worked as a clerk in the very same company where Brigette was pursuing a summer job. He was a master at cracking silly jokes, forging bonds and laughter in every situation, making fun of pain and disaster, creating a trap and then laughing at it. Rio excelled in the art of cultivating happiness. He was happy all the time. When the boss shouted at him, he laughed; when he broke his leg, he laughed; when he was beaten in a street fight, he laughed out loud; when he was hungry, he laughed, and he laughed when he was sad.

Brigette found his moods mesmerising. She was drawn to him like a magnet. She loved being with him. Rio took her for a coffee, later for a meal and then for a vacation, to buy new clothes; all at Brigette's expense. She kept giving, and enjoyed every bit of her power to give. She never pursued her Master's degree, and instead took up a job to be a provider. Rio would comfortably while away his time as Brigette worked hard and took care of all his mundane needs: a nice watch, a shirt, shoes, a few beers. Rio was comfortable being lazy and a pauper. She was okay being the breadwinner and a giver.

This went on for three long years, until Jennifer was born. Rio's irresponsible and casual attitude started to make her angry. His laughter without reason, his perpetual smile, his moods, his constant and loud chatter, his stupid jokes and his callousness started to irritate her immensely.

While at the office, she found herself constantly worrying about her daughter, Jennifer, at home there were demands and further demands, the demands of the infant and the demands of a rogue. She tolerated it for months together as Rio cared for the baby when she was at work. To begin with, Rio tried to change. He quit smoking and limited his alcohol consumption to weekends. He spent a lot of time with the baby, watching her grow. The rest of the time, he spent indulging in his new found love—yoga. He would get into weird postures, remaining in each posture for hours, performing breathing exercises, chanting out aloud, creating unheard of sounds and sitting idle, cross-legged, motionless with his eyes closed. For Brigette, this fulfilled no idea of an ideal spouse.

She was angry. Rio shrugged off all financial responsibilities. He had no valour, no drive. He pretended to live at a higher plane, and at her cost and at the cost of her child's destiny. After the household chores were over, she lay in bed like a vegetable with an unbearable migraine, which had become her constant companion. Rio had also started becoming restless. A loveless home, a demanding infant, a sick, tired and angry wife: all this started taking a toll on him. One fine morning, he packed his luggage neatly in a backpack, took all the money lying in the locker and disappeared.

Brigette felt relieved. She quit her job and nursed Jennifer with her fast-dwindling, meagre savings. It was just the two of them now. Rio, meanwhile, took off on a random ship to India, which sailed for Port of Madras and made his way to Auroville; a global village being built in South India based on the ideals of Shri Aurobindo, a Bengali saint, and Mother, Aurobindo's life-long French associate. He wrote home long letters from Auroville, mentioning how happy he was with his ashram mates, building an ideal city in which humanity could thrive, a city based on the principles of love and brotherhood of all nationalities, races and religions. In the beginning, she enthusiastically read these long vivid descriptions of his joy and his newfound peace, but soon she started becoming disillusioned with them, tired of their trite repetitiveness. She began tearing and throwing them in the dustbin, even without slitting them open. She never replied or even acknowledged these testimonies. After a few months the letters stopped. She became lonely again and Jennifer became her world. Jennifer fully occupied her, and the migraines began to get more bearable.

This went on for a year, when she fast realised that she no longer had money to sustain them, not even for a month. She desperately needed a job. It was not hard to find the job of an accountant. Every company, every large establishment, needed one. She started looking through job vacancy columns in the newspapers.

Brigette had been so engrossed with the baby that she had discontinued the daily newspaper; the news had no meaning in their existence. But now she needed it, and found herself searching for scraps. After a few unsuccessful attempts, she found mention of a steel company which was hiring. It was a large company with a presence all over Europe. She was pleasantly surprised to know that the Founder and Chief Executive Officer of the company was personally taking the interviews.

When she got there, she found a large number of people assembled for various jobs. It was a buzzing office, which seemed to only be expanding, since it appeared that they were hiring a whole lot of people.

The way the interviews were being conducted was also interesting. The interview committee interacted with the job seekers for a fairly long time, checking their qualifications, skills and aptitude. Afterwards, the CEO met the job seeker and offered them the placement. Once the placement was decided, the pay package was decided in another interaction with another set of executives.

Brigette met the CEO after completing a long deliberation with the other interviewers on a variety of subjects and skills. The CEO was a handsome, young Indian with pleasant manners. He made her feel very comfortable. What started as an exchange of pleasantries soon became an intense dialogue, where each was trying to know more about the other. Brigette had a feeling of being empowered in the presence of the CEO.

'You are a very good candidate, but not just for our finance,' he ultimately said. 'I have another offer to make. My personal assistant is moving on, would you like to take his job? I want an accountant to run my personal office.'

You will be expected to give "time" the same value as we give to money. You must use your time, and mine as an investment to connect to the right people and for the right task. This job will not only have a higher pay scale, but will also make better use of your skills and be more rewarding' he added.

Brigette had never wanted a high-intensity job. She wanted a job only to support her baby, who needed more time and more care. But something deep within her made her suddenly say, 'Yes.' She said it slowly, but firmly. She followed this up with a sharp intake of breath... a montage of her past rushed through her brains like a whistling engine.

'But I have a problem,' she spoke in a haste, not really wanting to announce her status as a single parent, 'I have a daughter and I am the only one taking care of her.'

'This is not a problem but a pleasure,' replied the CEO instantaneously. Brigette suddenly had a feeling of warmth around him. She had fallen in love with the man she was expected to serve.

Working for Saraswati was not work for her. It was much more intense. She had to control his time, his schedules, his meetings, his calls, his visitors and his visits. She had to be totally engrossed to do this job. For a few days, she left Jennifer with her landlady, a helpful woman. After getting her salary in advance, she started using the services of a baby sitter. She took Jennifer to office with her when Saraswati was away travelling, and when her work was not too taxing. Here, Jennifer moved from the arms of one colleague to another, until Brigette finished work.

One day, Saraswati came to office unscheduled due to a cancelled flight and met Jennifer. Very quickly, they got chummy and Saraswati took the child to his house, wanting Jennifer to meet his little daughter, asking Brigette to pick her up when she was done.

Saraswati lived in a fairly large house in an elite neighbourhood, a few blocks away from the office. Here, Jennifer met Saraswati's wife, Usha. His daughter Neha and Jennifer had already become chums and were playing as if they had known each other for ages.

Saraswati and Usha insisted that Brigette stay back for dinner. Brigette noticed that Usha was a devoted wife, and she spoke rather softly. She was also frail and got exhausted quickly. The house had to effectively be run by housekeepers, closely supervised by Ramlal, an elderly head cook. Sridhar and Ruzbeh, Saraswati's friends and partners, also joined them for dinner. The four of them had a long evening, with Usha frequently moving in and out to check on the children.

Neha was the same age as Jennifer. Both were yet to be enrolled in school. An arrangement was arrived at; every morning Brigette would leave Jennifer at Saraswati's house before heading to work. When work was done, she would pick her up on the way back from office. Jennifer would spend the day with Neha. It suited Usha well, as this provided company to Neha and gave her some rest during the day. That night, Brigette left Saraswati's home carrying a sleeping Jennifer in her arms, much relieved and much more committed to her boss and his company.

For Saraswati, Brigette was a boon. She was a good personal secretary, accounting each hour and every minute of Saraswati's time and putting it to the best possible use. His meetings were now better scheduled and better timed. His business interactions were more targeted and productive. He had more time for factory visits, more time to sit at the drawing board. Saraswati suddenly found himself more efficient; his work output improved for the quantum of time spent on various activities. Brigette would audit the time management every week. Saraswati met more professionals, made better deals, became more involved in project planning and still had time to read large documents, sit with the planners, monitor R&D initiatives, play golf with his legal team and have long three-course dinners with the bankers. He was also travelling more, all over the globe, to pick up closed foundries and steel mills. He was acquiring many more establishments, making better deals with labour, owners and financial institutions. He was choosing best of the legal teams and they were making better cases for takeover. His team quickly brought in the state-of-the-art technology and re-ignited mills that had been closed for months altogether, all in no time. Soon he was being invited by governments to takeover and turn around struggling public sector mills that had emerged during communist regimes. Saraswati was producing all kinds of steel, all over the world.

Even as he grew in business, his days became more leisurely. He could now squeeze in time for the gym twice a week, go for long drives with Neha and Jennifer, take them for picnics, play inconsequential games with them, read them story books, take them to the theatre and help Usha in the kitchen. They were now visiting the local Indian temple for every festival and were participating in elaborate pujas. Life had suddenly become more interesting, balanced, more fruitful and more rewarding.

Jennifer and Neha too had become inseparable. On each working day, Jennifer would be dressed and ready even before Brigette was. They would drive together to Saraswati's house to leave her with Neha and Usha. Brigette often baked cakes and brought them over to Usha, who eagerly looked forward to Brigette's arrival. She would hand over the prasad from the day's puja and then they took their morning tea together. A highly-spiced, milky, strong tea with an extra helping of sugar. For Brigette, the tea and the prasad soon started compensating for breakfast.

Brigette would be the first to reach office. She would rework on the daily schedule, keep redressing the agenda for each meeting and would then collect the resume and cards of each person that Saraswati would meet during the day. She would take note of the action points of each meeting and each phone call to utilise these for monitoring and for future deliberations.

Daily, she would meet Saraswati as he entered the portico of the office. By the time he reached his room using the elevator and traversing the long corridor, Brigette would have already given him the plan for the day. After each interaction ended, she would hand over her extensive notes. Brigette would again meet him at the end of the day to have a complete debriefing and make plans for the next.

Brigette would be the last to leave office, after making action points and passing them on to the respective departments, getting agendas, drawing minutes, keeping a tab on the register for visitors and telephone calls and closing requests for appointments. Due to her training as an accountant, she never left the office unless she had closed all accounts and the day's ledgers. She used her training and experience of accounts in managing time as the fundamental and most prime of all resources.

When she closed her office and reached Saraswati's house to pick Jennifer, she would find Sridhar and Ruzbeh already there. They would usually be found discussing plans and projections in an informal setting, cracking jokes, recalling their college mates and having drinks with oily and fried side-dishes, all vegetarian. They took their whisky with soda, compromising the taste of most expensive single malts. Brigette and Usha would also join them. Brigette attentively listened to the conversation, and Usha would move in and out, coordinating dinner and bringing in more and more side dishes. By the time they were done, it would already be late. Brigette would be pushed to dine with them. Later, she would pick up Jennifer, who would be sleeping in an embrace with Neha, and carry her in her arms to the car. This happened every single day, unless Saraswati was travelling. On those days, Brigette would spend some time with Neha, Usha and Jennifer, and take a reluctant Jennifer home early. Jennifer's growing comfort, and the love showered by Usha and Neha provided her baby with an extended family. She herself now had a secure and well-paying job, making her confident and decisive. In time, she also gained weight and had to wake up early to go for a jog, before Jennifer woke up and the day began.

Saraswati was so happy with the way things were going that he gave Brigette three increments, all within a single year! Her salary now was at par with the heads of departments; he even made her a shareholder by giving her a few shares of the company. Every six months, she would get a few more shares as a bonus.

The company was doing very well and their share value rose every single day as the stock market opened up. The company policy also provided for a substantial dividend, bonus shares and rights issues. Brigette also used a major portion of her savings in buying more and more shares of the growing company. She soon had her own apartment, a new car and enough savings to secure a reasonably good life for herself and Jennifer. But still, Brigette desired more. She wanted to forget her poverty-stricken past, make it seem like a distant nightmare. She wanted to grow out of it, fully and completely. She wanted Jennifer never to have financial problems. She wanted her daughter to live well, live comfortably, just as the children of the rich.

On weekends, she would spend time with Jennifer. One day, she took Jennifer for a drive to a remote village in the Black Forest. She was going home after more than a decade. She was surprised to see her grandmother alive, as if waiting all along for her return. A large gathering of her cousins and the impoverished, dull-headed children took turns to have a close look at the car in which she had driven in.

After this, she took Jennifer to the village, almost every weekend taking gifts, toys and clothes for her poor cousins and their families. She purchased a large house abandoned by an erstwhile baron in the centre of the village at a bargain; the mansion was situated adjoining the church and Brigette remodelled it to be a good residence for her grandmother. She employed three attenders to take care and nurse her ailing grandmother. She ensured that the house was well-stocked and that her grandmother was comfortable. Now, her visits to the Black Forest became less frequent. She made a corpus to provide income for her grandmother every month. After that, she once again severed all connections with the past, a past she had never considered hers, the shadows of which she hoped would never ever fall even remotely on Jennifer.

By the time it came for the kids to go to school, Saraswati had already decided that Neha would be home-schooled for some weird reason. And so it was that both Neha and Jennifer were learning from the comfort of their home. Tutors came to teach them the 3R's—reading, writing and arithmetic. Saraswati had taken a bigger house in the next block. This one had a swimming pool, a gymnasium and a play area. Everything was chalked out for Neha and Jennifer within the four walls of the house and they hardly stepped out. Later, Neha started taking Bharatnatyam classes organised in the local temple and Jennifer, adamant about it, enrolled for ballet.

But they both soon gravitated towards Bharatnatyam, followed by piano tuitions. Both turned out to be good swimmers as well. When they had to take public exams, they earned brilliant grades.

They had few other friends. Ruzbeh's son, Kiran, was the only boy who they really knew. He was a year older to them and often visited Saraswati's house. He went to the neighbourhood school. Soon, he too was taking classes in Bharatnatyam and piano. The girls joined him to learn fencing, an agile sport, which provided them enough exercise and finally, ample friends outside their twosome life.

Saraswati had to take off for more than a month when his father died in India. Brigette virtually ran his house as well his office. She was often consulted by Sridhar and Ruzbeh while taking important financial and operational decisions. She would make an international call to Saraswati every night to apprise him of the minutest details and take instructions. During his long absence, the company was running as if he had never left. When Saraswati returned, he quickly resumed his work.

Brigette was inducted as a Director in the company and became its fourth pillar. Things were going just fine. Days, months and years passed and Brigette's world revolved around Saraswati, Usha, Neha, Jennifer, Saraswati's company and Saraswati's friends. It was very comfortable, but very repetitive. And then, one day, everything changed.

Usha was more frail and tired than ever before. Her blood pressure was perpetually low and she could not exert herself to do the barest minimum. Brigette was always there to help, and to provide her company, support and later to accompany her to various hospitals. For Saraswati, Usha's health became a real cause of worry. Various ailments confronted her in close succession and her frail body had started to give way. She now confined herself to her room and stayed mostly in bed.

Now Brigette was doing for Neha what Usha had done for

Jennifer all these years. Taking them shopping, the weekend trips to the theatre, driving them to the temple, checking on their academic progress, and taking care of the various needs and emotions of the two girls who were entering puberty. Due to her deteriorating health, Usha had to be admitted to the hospital often. She would get better, and then suddenly, she would need to be put back to emergency care, making both time and life rather precarious.

She was now restless, tired of her existence, done with her body and mind, and fast consumed by a sense of worthlessness. What worried her was that Neha often woke up in the middle of the night, violently shaken from a horrific dream of being surrounded by vultures. She described them as large, ugly and looming birds, holding ripped flesh in their beaks, blood dripping from their crest, looking at her with their fierce eyes. Usha would try to console a frightened, howling Neha by embracing her closely. This would comfort Neha and she would slowly fall back to sleep. Usha however, remained awake for the rest of the night, trying to decipher the meaning of these deadly dreams. She often told Saraswati of the ominous dreams that Neha was repeatedly being tormented by.

One devastating day, Usha died in her sleep in a hospital bed with only Brigette by her side, breathing her last as Saraswati returned hurriedly from a project site. It looked as if he had already contemplated that this would happen, sooner rather than later. He was emotionless, silent and pale. Usha's death was followed by numbness, prolonged rituals and another long visit to India. Sridhar accompanied him for all the rituals and the journeys back home. This time, Saraswati did not want to take international calls and evening briefings. He left everything

to Brigette and Ruzbeh. This was the first time that Neha and Jennifer were kept apart for a long spell. Jennifer was shaken by the death of someone so close to her.

It took a long time for Saraswati to come to terms with his lonely existence. Now he was a single parent to Neha, and just a father figure in the household. He had Brigette, and she provided him with necessary support. She had to take charge both at home as well as at the office. She had to be a co-parent to Neha. The girls slowly got back to their regular routines. Kiran, too, was often present to given them company and in dealing with their grief, they gradually became a threesome.

Saraswati had never dealt with personal expenses. He had never shopped. He had never carried a wallet, never used a credit card. Now Brigette had to rope herself into everything and anything that happened to Saraswati. She paid his bills, bought him clothes and other essentials, lugged groceries for his house, took care of Neha, paid the household staff, ensured maintenance of his house and also managed his office. Her days were long, even though she now had a team of helpers to do the mundane work while she was a decision-maker. But it comforted her to be Saraswati's closest associate.

When Saraswati resumed office, he totally immersed himself in work. He often consulted Brigette, wanted her always by his side. They often drove together to office and then back home. She decided on what he would wear, his diet and was there during weekends as well. They took the children for picnics to Disneyland together and to the movies. They often dined together. Her own house was just a refuge for the night, where she and Jennifer would sleep. The rest of the time, Jennifer was with Neha, and she herself was with Saraswati.

Then one day, the inevitable happened. Brigette and Saraswati made love to each other. After a long long time, she felt the warmth of a man, one she felt connected to, a man whom she deserved, whom Jennifer deserved.

And then, Brigette and Saraswati were inseparable. They travelled for business and stayed in adjoining rooms. In all his business meetings, client interactions, board meetings, dinners with buyers and interactions with the authorities, she was there with him. Often silent, often quiet, but deeply observant. She had now accumulated sizable shares in the company, and the company was growing at a phenomenal rate.

Travel was frequent. They had plants all over the globe. They had offices in all major cities of the world. The world had become a family, and they had a presence everywhere. They travelled the world together.

Soon, it was their company and not his alone. Even though Saraswati was called the 'The Steel King' of the largest steel company in the world.

They were both now called in for formal interactions with heads of states. They were in the list of invitees to the White House for business meets. They were invited to talk in various forums and in innumerable summits for business leaders.

Brigette's village school was now being run by her. Her accountancy college had a chair in her name. Life for her was a fairy tale, but the more she grew in stature, the more her desires accelerated.

She wanted nothing for herself. Now, it was all about Jennifer. It was Jennifer for whom she had woven this canvas. Her struggle, her hard work, her involvement, her life was now solely to ensure that Jennifer would have a formidable place in the universe.

5

Theatre of the Absurd

When the time for pursuing college education came, Saraswati eschewed regular college for Neha, opting instead to let her sign up for distance education. Brigette was dismayed at his choice, although it was only for Neha and not Jennifer. It was completely unacceptable to her and she said as much.

She had always wanted Jennifer to go to a regular college, and later, study in the best of business management schools. She could afford to give her the best possible education, even arrange for her to study in any of the Ivy League Universities. Brigette was unwilling to compromise, even if it meant that Jennifer had to part ways with Neha.

Jennifer too had a desire to go to college. But she wanted to pursue theatre, which was not what Brigette had dreamt for her. Theatre was not promising, not in terms of a secure future. A career in fine arts, music, dramatics and dance had limitations, she felt. Most students pursued these streams in order to merely remain in them, she argued. First as students and later as teachers!

Not many made big money, not many had a career and not many became rich and successful! It was a hand-to-mouth existence, she told Jennifer. Having been brought up so luxuriously, this was not an ideal choice for Jennifer. For Brigette, who had high aspirations for her daughter, this was not a life at all.

However, Jennifer was insistent on pursuing her dreams, and for the first time, she dug her heels in and was adamant. Helpless and unable to change her daughter's aspirations, Brigette consulted Sridhar and his horoscope.

Date, place and time of birth provided the building blocks for constructing the chart of Jennifer's destiny. When Sridhar looked at the chart, he instinctively compared it with that of Neha's, which he remembered by heart. Jennifer has a very comfortable fourth, fifth and seventh house, he informed Brigette. She would have a beautiful home, a loving spouse and healthy children. She would live happily and enjoy a contented life.

However, he kept to himself what Neha's horoscope spelt out for her. Neha's would be a roller-coaster ride. She would ascend great heights followed by even greater falls; this would happen time and again, and in unstoppable succession. Neha was bestowed with a powerful tenth, second and third house, giving her name, fame and wealth, but not necessarily joy, happiness and peace. Jennifer's life was guided by a strong peaceful Jupiter, while Neha's was governed by Rahu, the headless, vibrant, dragon rigorously flapping its tail.

Brigette was devastated by Sridhar's predictions for Jennifer's future. As far as she was concerned, a happy life without success was worthless. Happiness was only a state of mind, it could be found and manifested. But success is vital. Excellence is mandatory. It provides one with an edge. What is the purpose of a

life without this edge—without authority and without excellence?

Brigette made a quick trip to the Black Forest. Her grandmother had died and the house she had lived in was now a shelter for orphans. For a long time now, Brigette had been paying for the boarding, lodging and education of orphans not only from her village, but from the entire county. She went to the quiet little village church adjoining the house and prayed fervently. She always found peace and calm in the church, and her prayers helped her to keep her hopes alive. She met up with the village priest and told him about her predicament. All he said was that she had to be patient with Jennifer. 'Give her some time and things will be fine,' he said. Brigette walked out of the church feeling just a little lighter, but not fully soothed.

That night, Brigette was reminded of Rio. She woke up on hearing the uncontrolled and vehement laughter of the rogue. He was teasing her, troubling her, not permitting her to sleep! She got up and went to Jennifer's room and found her fast asleep. Suddenly, she felt tears rolling down her cheeks.

By now, Rio must have become a senior member of the Aurobindo Ashram. He might have become a preacher of a new world order. Perhaps he had returned to Berlin, gotten married and was living with his new family; his wife and their children. Happily! Brigette was now sobbing uncontrollably, weeping and wailing. She sobbed throughout the night.

Oblivious to her mother's cries of pain, Jennifer slept on. She was in deep slumber with a smile on her face... as if nothing had changed. The following month, Jennifer joined an undergraduate course in theatre at a renowned school of fine arts in Milan, leaving Brigette alone in their large, empty mansion. Her daughter had flown the coop, unmindful of Brigette's pleas. Now the nest was empty, leaving only Saraswati and Neha.

From the very beginning of their relationship when she had been a little girl, Saraswati had been extremely protective of Neha. He never liked even discussing it with anybody. Brigette's role was to only assist him, never to offer advice, not when it came to Neha. After Usha's death, the only person who knew method in the madness surrounding Neha's upbringing was probably Sridhar. Neha never went to a regular school. Other than Jennifer and Kiran, she hardly had any other friends. She pursued higher education from a distance, learning from books and screens. After her initial training in Bharatanatyam, the only reason for her to step out of the house was to go to the private golf range that Saraswati had acquired in the outskirts of the city. It had a long driving range, with a few landscaped obstacles and a putting green.

In the beginning, Brigette thought that this was probably the way all within the Indian community raised their children. But the current generation of Indians in Germany were studying in the best of schools and colleges. They easily mingled with the local youth, and many of them even married outside their communities and culture. They were open-minded and wished to be part of the mainstream with a vengeance. Neha was different; unexposed, alone and aloof, barely interacting with the outside world, living under a protective membrane in an absurd world created for her by her father.

Lately, Saraswati was spending more time with Neha. He would go with her to the driving range and take her along when he travelled, leaving Brigette with a vaster void in her life. On his travels, he took Neha to meet affluent families from India who were spread across the world. During summers, they would

pack up for weeks together to play golf in the most sought-after golf circuits. Golf took them to the most beautiful places in the world, and there they met and befriended the most successful, the most powerful and the wealthiest of people. Neha met young men from business houses, films, media and politics; the second and third generations of the greatest global achievers and wealth makers.

During the rest of her time, Neha would be buried in her books: an odd collection of philosophy, psychology, travelogues, biographies and spiritual literature of varied religions and cults. She also studied space science, particle physics, biochemistry, genetic engineering and information technology. Probably the absence of a regimented regular college permitted her to swim across varied streams of knowledge and wisdom with ease.

Expecting the unexpected and yet unwilling to allow uncertainty, Saraswati had engaged the best of matchmakers to search for the most suitable groom for his princess, a real prince, for the most eligible young Indian girl—his only child and his entire world! Sridhar would regularly be bombarded by hundreds of horoscopes, asking to be matched with that of Neha's. There would often be guests at home , arriving with their well-groomed sons to meet the mysterious daughter. On most of these occasions, Brigette would return home after meticulously arranging the meetings, leaving the father and daughter alone with the guests.

Brigette had never felt so helpless in her life. Her relationship with Saraswati was restricted to providing physical comfort, that too occasionally. There was no romance, no thrill. While Saraswati was completely absorbed in finding a suitable boy for his daughter, she would be alone most evenings and most weekends too. She often thought about Jennifer, missing her, even crying for her. Lately, Rio had also started to show up in her dreams. She thought of a smiling Rio, a laughing Rio, just as he was in the initial days of their courtship. She wanted to find some happiness and peace from her first and only real love.

Neha met with the owner of a large business house in India, as well as his two sons. Both were well educated, having graduated from renowned business schools, and were already assisting their father in business. They showed terrific promise, Saraswati told her. One had a deep drive for money and the other a deeper thirst for success in Bollywood, the thriving film industry based in Bombay. One had poise and the other had charm.

Neha made a quick trip to Milan to be with Jennifer, to discuss and deliberate upon the various proposals she had received.

When she returned, she had made up her mind. It would be a game of golf that would decide her life-mate. Everything else would be in sync with her father's wishes. According to her, golf brought out the real character of humans: their drive, the way they faced obstacles, the manner in which they managed initial successes and mistakes, and above all, how they finished and took their triumph or the burden of defeat to the next hole! One could really gauge the handicap of people, a person's instincts and their behaviour from the game. Finally, golf would also provide her with a chance for long, scenic walks in the fresh air, and an opportunity to engage in stimulating conversation. Yes, the golf course would be the turf where Neha would decide who she would spend the rest of her life with.

She made many more trips to Milan since she had very little time to herself, and would soon be taking on the role of a bride and a daughter-in-law. She would have to be a queen with

more wealth and more privileges than what her father could ever provide.

As the days passed, Neha became quiet, afraid and aloof. To her it felt as if time was running out, as if she was being isolated, surrounded and cornered, with no escape. She wanted to be with Jennifer all the time. Brigette had never seen Neha so restless. She ate less, slept more and often took endless walks in the garden. Sometimes, she would swim for hours together and, at other times, she would be looking out at the empty skies vacantly, without any purpose.

Then, one fine morning, she announced aloud to Saraswati—in the presence of Sridhar, Brigette and Ruzbeh—that she wanted a break. She would not resist any match fixed by Saraswati. She would attempt to be a devoted wife, just as her mother had been. She would never digress from the wishes of her father or the path he had laid out for her. But all this could happen only after she had had a taste of life. She wanted to be free for a few months. She wanted to travel, meet people and see the world. She wanted to be out of the sheltered cocoon that this life provided, she wanted to be less pinned to the board for once.

Saraswati was heartbroken. His worst fears had taken flight. It was now his turn to go for long walks and look endlessly into the open skies. He was scared that his daughter might break free, find that freedom intoxicating and decide not to settle for the drudgery of marriage and domesticity.

Neha, on the other hand, was now at peace. She had articulated her sole wish to her father, and she knew that he would not turn it down. A few days later, Saraswati spent a long evening with Sridhar. After detailed discussions, it was decided that Neha would have her way. But there would be a few conditions attached to it: Jennifer would have to accompany her wherever she went. Neha had to keep Sridhar informed of all her movements. She would not get into drugs—at any cost—and, she was never ever to befriend any boys.

Neha laughed when Sridhar spelt out the conditions to her. She was pleased to have Jennifer's company and sharing her whereabouts was no big deal. The conditions regarding drugs and boys were hilarious and meaningless. It was as if she was a child who was being forbidden to take a chocolate. She suddenly felt as if her father was more of a child, someone who could be so easily persuaded and bluffed. For now, Sridhar was the only bridge between Neha and Saraswati, with very little direct communication between father and daughter. Surprisingly, Brigette was not even consulted.

The next week, Neha was off to Milan with her passport, a credit card and a meticulously planned travel itinerary. She carried no baggage.

6

The Flying Carpet

After spending a few days in Milan, Neha and Jennifer set off on their voyage across the world. They decided to hop over the major cities of Europe, as they had already visited most of them with their parents. Their first stop was at Vardo, where they spent many nights without a sunset. The town was extremely cold and windy; the landscape was devoid of trees and shrubs and rather bleak. They found it difficult to fall asleep due to the omnipresent sunlight. It took them several days to reset their body clocks.

Their next port of call was Russia, a country which had been carved out of the Soviet Union that had once spread across the continents of Europe and Asia. They boarded the famous Trans-Siberian Railways, the world's longest railway, built by the czars to restore and govern their vast empire. They hopped in and out at different stations in this vast country's picturesque, sparsely-populated towns. These little towns were so beautiful, almost untouched by the passage of time, shelved in old-world charm.

The train took them from Russia to Beijing after a seemingly endless journey, covering thousands of miles through Mongolia. It felt as if they had entered a different world, almost a new planet, where humans had just landed and were making efforts to establish a new civilisation.

The People's Republic of China was unlike anywhere they had ever been before. Like Russia, it was a Communist country, and the iron fist of the government ruled over every aspect of its citizen's lives. Neha was confused. Communism was supposed to spread equality among people, and in theory, that was good. But after seeing the lack of freedom among people of Russia and China, and their lack of privacy, she wondered whether capitalism, with all its flaws, was not a better option! And democracy gave people the right to protest, the right to speak. What she had seen in Communist nations was far from utopia. Egalitarianism and similar marvels for which it had been envisaged and established after enormous struggle and turmoil seemed lost. However, amidst this ideological conflict, China's growth was phenomenal and its economy was marching to glory by utilising market economy, private wealth and for that matter, everything that was anathema to Communism, other than a totalitarian regime.

From Beijing, they travelled via rail and road to reach Lhasa, the beautiful capital of Tibet, where a serene Buddhist culture thrived under the shadows of the great Himalayan peaks. The tranquil atmosphere of Lhasa and the sight of Buddhist monks calmly going about their day-to-day lives was a refreshing and uplifting change from the grimness they had seen in urban habitations. The beauty of the Himalayan surroundings, the peaceful and serenely luminescent monasteries, and the all-pervading sense of spirituality was a salve for their souls. Neha felt she had reached her destination. Jennifer had to literally force her to continue the rest of their journey.

Finally, they entered India via Bhutan, a landlocked country with a unique identity and culture. The kingdom of Bhutan was again a Buddhist country, and it seemed untouched by the twentieth century. It was a different world altogether, almost a Shangri-La; so beautiful and so quaint.

After touching base on Indian soil, they journeyed to Nepal, to trek to the Everest base camp. It was a long, tedious trek with many halts in charming monasteries and bed-and-breakfast in European cafés that had mushroomed all across the route. Their Sherpa guide had organised their entire gear on rent. He was an experienced guide who knew the lay of the land and for an extra tip, regaled them with stories of his unique experiences dealing with trekkers from across the world.

As she trudged along the trail, Neha was astonished that mankind had conquered the top of the world in the mid-1950s, and then, within a few years, had even landed two men on the moon. Such giant leaps for humanity, and both almost in succession was amazing. She was equally astonished to learn that there could be higher peaks deep within the oceans and the seas, which were still unexplored. But for now, she was content to feast her eyes on the magnificent spectacle of the ice-capped peaks of the world's highest mountain range.

It made her feel small. Human beings seemed so insignificant in the face of the majesty of nature.

Neha picked up a new habit. She would read the local newspaper of every city she visited, back-to-back, immersing herself in the ethos of the place. Neha and Jennifer met many people during their journey. They discovered lingering languages, unique civilisations, varied cultures and strange customs. Each country's landscape, history, monuments, cuisine and culture had so much to offer, and there was so much they could learn. However, they saw how the capitalist-industrial society wanted all to favour the economy of scale and apply the time-tested laws of market segmentation, because a diverse world is not a panacea for the markets.

From Kathmandu, they went to war-torn Pakistan. From there, they wound their way to Afghanistan, Iran and Iraq, frightening Sridhar to such an extent that he persuaded them to take the first flight from Baghdad to New Delhi. But in the little time they spent there, Neha saw varying shades of the monotheistic religions, each so different, so diverse and so unique and yet, so overshadowed by a few that made them run like a war machine. All that brutality in the name of a religion that was born to end all conflicts, inequalities and superstitions.

Returning to India was like homecoming for Neha. She visited Hisar, the land of her forefathers, and met a multitude of cousins, uncles, aunts and their equally large families. She felt as if she belonged there; as if she had never lived in Germany and had always been here, among her extended family and had not moved an inch. She went to Lady Hardinge Medical College, curious to see the place where her father was born.

They then headed to Bombay, the financial capital, a city that the British had once received as dowry from the Dutch. Bombay seemed so different and vibrant in comparison to what little they had seen of India. It was crowded, busy and dotted with tall buildings. The city was alive and jam-packed, its hustle-bustle never ending.

After visiting Goa and enjoying its golden beaches and lush

greenery, they went to Madras, the gateway to South India. Madras lay on the Coromandel Coast, and they found it to be a far more traditional and old-fashioned city as compared to Bombay. They spent a few days in Madras, visiting magnificent temples, built thousands of years ago at Mahabalipuram. They were awestruck by the marvels of ancient engineering. These temples had been constructed by placing huge stones, one over the other, in an era when cranes were non-existent, and had been cemented with lime to last for centuries.

They then went to the little town of Vaitheeswaran Koil to meet another clan, Sridhar's family. They were eagerly waiting to see Neha, and treated her like their own granddaughter. It was all so different from Germany. Here, people were loud, affectionate and very curious. In Germany, Neha had always felt and even internalised a restrain when interacting with other people. No one asked personal questions in Germany, but in India, personal space was not a time-worn concept. People surrounded you all the time, bombarded you with all sorts of questions, and did so innocently. Nevertheless, Neha did love her newfound family. She was overwhelmed by their warmth and affection.

Their visit to Auroville was the only time Jennifer wanted to be left alone. She was not searching for spiritual fulfilment, but for a single person, wanting to tie together the thread of her life. For one entire week, she wandered endlessly, while Neha meditated in the magnificent spherical meditation hall with its white spreads, where a magnificent crystal glowed, bathed in the direct beams of sunlight. Neha was surprised that she could sit here motionless, for hours together, watching her thoughts and then, gradually channelling and focusing them, as if she'd always known how to. For the first time in her life, she felt that she was watching her mind, her body and her soul as an outsider, feeling much lighter and so much more at peace.

Neha knew why Jennifer was so restless. She knew what Jennifer was looking for. But she never said anything. It was Jennifer's quest, her turbulence, and only she could take a call in this matter and unravel the mysteries of her life. Neha never found out if Jennifer ever met her father, or if she saw him and left without telling him who she was!

Very soon, Jennifer too was more at peace. They both had felt something like tranquillity, of being more complete. The sylvan surroundings of Auroville gave them a chance to recognise their real selves. It was like nirvana: a blend of bliss and fulfilment, which became an integral part of them for the rest of their lives. Visiting Auroville and experiencing its utopian ideals had changed their lives for the better.

They left India, to embark on a journey to the new world of Americas. They came across folks who still lived as hunter-gatherers. They travelled through countries built and run by drug mafias, inhabited by the most fun-loving and fearless women in the world. On the other hand, New York was a world of its own. Thousands of people walked in and out of its busy lanes, visiting restaurants, travelling and working through its business houses. It had a vibrancy and energy they had not seen anywhere else in the world.

They went on a cruise to Alaska and were awed by the wind-swept beauty of its icy terrain: the snowy landscape, the crystal-clear lakes and the verdant alpine forests, like a slice of pristine paradise on earth. Neha was awestruck by the place because it was still so untouched by humans, still undestroyed. The ravages of pollution and human greed for development had

not yet overwhelmed this beautiful abode. It was a testament to how the world could be if humans learned to live with and respect nature.

And then it was time for the rugged beauty of South Africa. Africa was stunning. But while nature bloomed in all its magnificence, the spectacle of apartheid had cast a stain on its beauty. They spent many days experiencing the raw beauty of the African landscape and its wildlife, and simultaneously witnessing the ugliness of its widespread poverty. Why had poverty ravaged such a heavenly place? And why did humans discriminate on grounds of colour? These thoughts kept Neha awake at night as the crickets and other creatures of the night broke the still silence of the Dark Continent.

She and Jennifer reached Ibiza, the hedonistic island in the glittering Mediterranean Sea, on the last leg of their journey. Ibiza had the most happening nightlife in all of Europe. After the vast landscapes of Africa and the stillness of the nights spent in the wild, Ibiza was a cultural shock, raucously welcoming them back to 'civilisation'. As they mingled with the epicurean hordes that thronged the scenic island, Neha was ready to let her hair down and live in the moment... forget about all demands from life, living and humanity.

During the entire journey, it was Jennifer who had been more forthcoming, outgoing, friendly and lively. Neha had been silent, observant, quiet and laid-back. The 'no boys, no drug' regime had given her a vital power, and she stuck by it. The power of observation, assimilation and analysis. Whenever Jennifer delved into a long conversation with a newly-made friend, she became the observer. She noted vivid details of the conversations and descriptions of various places and diverse interactions in her diary. She was reminded of Socrates when she realised that knowledge is absorbed best through dialogue. Monologues, sermons and meetings have very little to do with the progress of the human mind.

Their travels around the world had taken them to islands, mountains, grasslands, dense forests and wind-swept deserts. The sheer diversity and disparity in the world was intriguing. Earth is home to all kinds of flowers, animals and human races—the so-called 'blacks', the 'whites', the 'yellows' and 'browns' and their various intermediate shades—made the human race an unending rainbow.

Western and eastern civilisation were the two poles, each dotted with an assortment of races, ethnicities and ethos in the vast canvas of human civilisation, each with their unique architecture, language, social structure, food, tools and costumes. The world was a salad bowl of cultures, slowly becoming a melting pot where identities were getting messed up and mixed up.

Neha observed with despair the wanton exploitation of the world's limited natural resources. Mining, deforestation, piles of waste, garbage and pollution were all too visible, and its impact was accelerating. To her it was as if mankind was in a race, making sure to kill this paradise by making it unsustainable and barren. By putting waste in somebody else's backyard, the predators were only postponing its intrusion into their own lives, ultimately making it all ugly, dark and beyond redemption.

The melting ice, disappearing islands, harsh winters, extreme temperatures, fast-disappearing freshwater, expanding deserts, the flight of top soil, contaminated food, shrinking habitation, threatened wildlife... all this loss had been discernible during their journey. Urban life, in most countries, was a nightmare

full of crime, drugs, desperation, exploitation, death and despair. Slums grew, engulfing cityscapes not only in poorer nations, but also in the neighbourhoods of advanced and prosperous cities in the west.

It had made them sad, and often despondent. But soon, a visit to a marvellous palace, a beautiful church, a vibrant discotheque, a friendly bookstore or seeing a laughing child, smelling the aroma of roasted coffee, hearing an old song playing in the background, touching a wild flower making its appearance on a vast patch of grass, a squirrel nibbling a nut, a monk with a broad smile, a dog running to his master or a walk on the beach would raise their spirits. It would make them forget all the ugliness, and they would momentarily believe that the world truly was a beautiful place. They would forget all the poverty, all the misery and all the sorrows slowly engulfing the world.

Jennifer and Neha travelled light, with barely any luggage. They procured whatever they needed and the leftovers were given to charity. Whenever they left a city, they left everything behind, except for the clothes they were wearing.

Her diary was the only material object that stayed with Neha till the end; even the books were donated once read. They had no cameras, and they took no photographs. Neha never wanted any of their memories to remain with her. Somewhere in her heart, she knew that these memories would lead to confusion and turmoil within the life she was already wedded to.

They spent most of their days travelling by public transport, observing, figuring out, assimilating and writing. They hardly ever had a sit-down meal. There was too much to see, feel and experience before these moments and this time became a distant memory in their past. At night, they would take off the only clothes they possessed to get into bed and sleep in each other's embrace, as they had been doing for years.

For Neha, after Usha's passing, it was Jennifer and her familiar body odour, whose contours and warmth provided safety, comfort and pleasure. They longed for these hours, which they had often been denied when Brigette or Saraswati had been around. To put aside this bond was probably going to be Neha's biggest challenge for the life to which she was quickly moving towards.

Except for a few moments when they felt lonely, cheated or distressed, travelling provided them with a sense of the oneness of life and gave them unparalleled joy. The very presence of each other brought so much fun and meaning to the entire experience. They had travelled the world together and had evolved as people; more knowledgeable about humanity, about the good and the bad, about how humans were in a race to destroy the world. They often wondered: could they do anything to make a difference?

Ibiza, the party island in the Mediterranean Sea off the eastern coast of Spain, was fast emerging as the most popular tourist destination in Spain, leaving behind Madrid, Barcelona, Seville, Granada, Cordoba, Valencia and all the other marvellous cities filled with historic monuments, museums, opera halls, churches, art galleries, sculptures, gardens, public parks and beautiful riverbanks. Youth from all over the world gravitated towards the beaches of Ibiza, taking short flights, cruise ships and even motor boats from the mainland. They were least interested in sampling the culture and history of mainland Spain; they wanted to indulge, engage in debauchery and party till they dropped. Ibiza was the 'it' destination as far as partying went!

The island was a treasure trove for party animals. There were cottages on the beach overlooking marvellous views of the golden

sands and turquoise waters, loud music that thumped through the night, and bodies full of rhythm. They went dancing, letting their hair down and forgetting all about the harsh realities of life. They consumed alcohol and drugs to transport them into a surreal world where fantasy ruled over reality.

During the day, it was just another sleepy fishing village. But when darkness descended, the town came alive with parties, dance, music and spirited souls. During the weekends, swarms of young men and women would roam the beaches, all looking for a good time, before they returned to their boring, humdrum routines.

Ibiza never slept. 'Bed and breakfast' labels were a misnomer here; nobody ever woke up in time for breakfast, since the kids were either too exhausted or, more likely, too hung over after partying all night! There were no early morning flights from Ibiza either, as the aviation business very well knew that the visitors would not be in any condition to wake up and make it on these flights after a frenetic night of partying and imbibing vice.

Neha and Jennifer spent many sleepless nights and somnolent days in Ibiza. After their whirlwind tour around the world, this seaside paradise was like another world... a world where they could let themselves loose and carefree, where no one was watching or judging. They could party the night away, swaying to the rhythmic beat of music, feeling carefree and happy. Neha knew that Ibiza was the final leg of their voyage, the last of their time together before they re-entered an uncertain world, a world of reality, of problems, of the day-to-day mundanities...

It was their last night on the island paradise. The beach party they had attended only ended well past midnight. There was a full moon in the dark sky and the sands gleamed silver against the black glittering sea as they made their way back to the cottage. Neha had joined Jennifer and a group of friends they had recently got acquainted with, to have a few drinks. She had not touched alcohol during the entire trip, but tonight had made an exception. She wanted to feel free, completely unfettered on this happy-go-lucky last night of her journey.

She had worked so hard for this journey, had literally begged her father for, and stolen from her destiny. It was a journey of discovery—of the world, of herself and of her relationships. This trip was virtually devoted to herself and Jennifer. She didn't want to leave any desire unfulfilled. She wanted to return to the real world refreshed, rejuvenated and contented.

On reaching the cottage, they took a shower and got ready to go to bed. The resort they were staying in was winding down; all the lights were being switched off and the last of the partygoers were being persuaded to return to their rooms. As she got into the bed, she heard the loud whirring of big machinery.

The parties invariably left tons of garbage on the beach. Beer cans, bottles, cigarette stubs, paper plates, napkins, silver foils, wasted food, needles, sanitary pads, used condoms, urine, vomit and sometimes, even shit. The municipal authorities of the city had a unique way of cleaning the beach. A huge amount of sand was dug from some undeveloped area, brought in on trucks and spread over the beaches where the parties were held, a thick layer to bury the muck. In the morning, once again, they had a clean beach, all ready for yet another party and yet another garbage dump to be buried by many more truckloads of sand. It was a vicious cycle of bad management with no viable solution at hand. Neha thought that this methodology was terribly short-sighted and its potential impact was unknown. How long could

this go on? How long could mankind hide its ugly deeds? How long could the beaches sustain this rape by humanity? How long would this go on before it became irreversible and before the beauty of these beaches were lost forever?

Now that the beach had been cleaned, the trucks were retreating, and it was quiet again. Neha and Jennifer had been tossing and turning in bed; they were restless and unable to sleep. Not having consumed alcohol in a long time, Neha was feeling dehydrated. She got up to drink some water. Looking out of the window, she stared at the empty beach; the sea was luminous in the silvery moonlight.

She opened the door to get some fresh air. She heard a sound and turned to find that Jennifer had woken up too and was standing behind her. They innocently walked out onto the open balcony. They sat there for a while, the moonlight lighting their uncovered torsos. They had only their skins to cover their soul. The silver-tipped waves crashed on the shore rhythmically, creating a primeval music of their own while the stars sparkled in the inky sky. After the loud thumping music, the crush of bodies and the smell of alcohol, dope and tobacco, now everything was calm, pristine and beautiful.

They gazed at each other, clasped hands and started walking towards the beach, the full moon illuminating their bare bodies. It was their last night of togetherness, their last night of freedom. They wet their feet in the water as the foamy waves washed up and recedded again.

Suddenly, they were charged with a flash, a burst of energy. Soon, they were running across the silver sands, stopping, walking, jumping, laughing, whistling, hissing, catcalling and caressing each other like two little girls, enjoying themselves with no one to watch, no one to check, no one to guide, no one to reprimand. The soft sand, the crisp and clean air, the cool breeze, the creamy waves and their moonlit bodies ushered in a magical feeling, something they had never felt or experienced before. They felt a strong attraction to each other, a chemistry that was beyond their understanding. They were lost in their own world, as if they were united in body, spirit and soul. They lost themselves to the magic at this enchanted spot under the star-studded sky as the sea lent a background score. A flash of light distracted them, as if someone had lit a match. They were momentarily distracted but they went back to exploring each other. They were blissfully unaware, caught up as they were in their newly discovered passion. But unbeknownst to them... somebody was around, somebody was watching them.

As dawn descended on the island, the sky turned light, streaked with pink, purple and orange, and soon the sun peeped over the horizon—a shimmering orange globe bathing the earth in its life-giving light. They lay there lazily on the beach, entwined in each other's arms, watching the sunrise as it bathed the beach in an otherworldly glow.

Neha suddenly got up, and Jennifer followed. They both headed back towards the cottage. First walking, then running away from the sun's harsh rays which was chasing them, exposing them. They collapsed on the bed exhausted and slept in each other's arms until well past lunch. As they hurriedly got ready, it was already time to catch a flight to Milan, leaving behind the most memorable, cherished moments of their lives. It was back to the real world...

7

Life's Eternal Cycle

The photograph published in *The New York Times* devastated Saraswati. Never before had he felt so helpless and remorseful. He became a different person overnight. He barely spoke and had lost all interest in the business. He became a shell of the man he used to be: broken, listless and disinterested in everything around him. The photograph changed his life, shattered him totally.

Kiran took upon himself the impossible task of erasing every shred of evidence, all possible copies of the scandalous photograph of Neha. It had to be tracked and removed from all photographic films and the memories of all computers to banish its existence. The photograph needed to go away at any cost. This was a blot on everything Saraswati had strived to build for his precious daughter.

As days passed, Saraswati would often be found in tears. It seemed as if all prospects of marriage of his daughter into a respectable family had vanished. Suddenly, from being the most-eligible and most courted girl, Neha had become an object of disgrace. She was persona non-grata. No respectable Indian family would touch her, not even with a bargepole. She was eminently unsuitable.

Saraswati was angry with everybody—Sridhar, Jennifer and Brigette—and would curse himself for having been so naïve and irresponsible. Brigette felt helpless in the face of these changed circumstances. She would often find herself at a loss for words and felt as if she was being treated as a suspect in a vicious plan to disgrace Neha and Saraswati and everything that they had worked for, dreamt and desired.

Neha, too, was in a state of shock. She did not have the courage to face her father, or to even make a call to apologise. She was not worried about herself; neither did she feel any sense of disgrace or of having done anything wrong. Her only worry was Saraswati, who she very well knew would be distressed and devastated due to the unhappy repercussions of this uncalled-for development. She didn't know how to face him. The thought of looking into his reproachful eyes made her shudder. She was not ashamed, but she felt terrible that her father had to suffer its consequences. How would she face him? That was her sole worry.

Meanwhile, the vultures were haunting her dreams. Bigger, deadlier and more frightening this time. But for the presence and soft embrace of Jennifer, she would have certainly collapsed from the horror of the vultures refusing to leave her.

She somehow gathered the courage to depart for home after a week, having given her father a little time to come to terms with the incident. Somewhere in her heart she knew that things would be just fine. She had not committed some grave mistake. In the modern world, it was not such a big deal. The incident was avoidable, but it was not unpardonable. Time would take care

of it, erase it from people's memories and heal the wound left by it. After all, 'Time' was a great healer and people had short memories. Saraswati would overcome the shock, and life would probably be better once he got over the incident, the photographs and all the unwelcome publicity that had come in its wake. She was also relieved at gaining a few more days of normalcy. It was a few more days of freedom before the matchmaking recommenced.

However, Saraswati was unable to come to terms with the scandal. His life had changed; it had turned upside down and he was unable to move forward or forget. He felt that his reputation was in tatters, his life was in tatters.

One fateful day, Saraswati requested that Brigette stay the night at his house. This was the first time he had made such a request. Past midnight, Brigette was woken by a sweating Saraswati; his whole body shaking and shivering. As she attempted to give him a glass of water, his body suddenly turned motionless and cold. He took his last breath in Brigette's arms. He was rushed to the hospital where they declared him dead on arrival.

Neha was woken up by a dreadful early morning call. Sridhar told her that Saraswati was extremely ill. A taxi and the earliest flight had already been booked for her. She was surprised to see Kiran at the airport to receive her. She knew that this was not a good omen. Things seemed to have gone dreadfully wrong.

As she entered the house, she found the large sitting room bare, devoid of any furniture. Flowers, the smell of incense, and tapes of Vedic mantras were being played, announcing her father's passing away as she slowly entered the house, overcome by a sense of dread. A lifeless Saraswati lay on the floor, covered with a white shroud.

There was no time to mourn. Everyone was impatiently waiting for Neha in order to begin the rituals for the death ceremony. Soon, the body was taken to the Hindu crematorium in an ambulance. A few cars accompanied it to the temple. Neha, Brigette and the other women stayed back at the temple while the men took the body to the crematorium. Jennifer had also joined them by now. Neha stood there, numb, in a state of shock. This was all her doing. Her father had died because of her. Could she ever overcome that guilt?

The pyre was lit by Sridhar, dressed in mourning white, his head tonsured. Saraswati's body was given back to nature in the form of its elements: fire, water, air, earth and ether. His body slowly burnt on the pyre till all that was left was ash, leaving no trace of his existence, other than memories of him and his deeds.

The next few days were spent in conducting further rituals and last rites, sedately greeting the hordes of people who had come to offer condolences. Saraswati was well-known and respected in Germany. People of stature came to place wreaths, even the German Chancellor came to pay his last respects. There were services held in the local church in memory of Saraswati. Several employees of the company from various corners of the world travelled all the way to Berlin to pay their tributes, and obituaries were published in all the leading newspapers of the world.

Neha paid a visit to India once again, carrying the urn holding Saraswati's ashes. The ashes were first taken to Hisar, where his relatives paid their respects. The President, Prime Minister, Chief Ministers and large business houses conveyed their condolences to this great son of India. The elder of the two Bombay boys also came and stayed with Neha for a day during her time of grieving. Nobody talked about the toxic photograph. It seemed as

if nobody was actually bothered by it. Neha was greatly relieved. She also felt her confidence slowly burgeoning. Could it all finally be behind her?

Ultimately, the urn was taken to the holy city of Haridwar, in the foothills of the Himalayas, to immerse the ashes in the holy Ganges. Neha was overcome with a desire to trek all the way to Gangotri to take the blessings of Chaudhary Baba, the man who had seen it all much before it actually happened. However, something prevented her from being adventurous again, and she forced herself to forgo this deep-seated desire. There will always be a next time, she told herself, postponing her meeting with the saint.

Once all the rituals were over, Sridhar and Neha returned to Germany, with a final prayer for the departed soul's moksha—his absolution from further cycles of birth and death, at the temple town of Rameshwaram at India's southernmost tip. The island town of Rameshwaram is deemed to be one of the holiest places in India, and one of the Char Dhams or four most revered pilgrimage centres in India.

When Neha returned to Germany, she found herself overwhelmed with the several demands of the business. The board had to be reconstituted, and a new chairman had to be elected. The compliance reports and accounts needed to be submitted to the authorities. Taxes had to be paid, transfer documents had to be signed and legal formalities were required to be completed as Neha took charge of the largest steel company in the world.

Neha did not have any training or any real expertise to run this sprawling business. She was not even mentally prepared to shoulder such a big responsibility. It was her future husband who was designed to be the real heir. But destiny and circumstance had taken an unexpected turn, and now she would have to take the helm without any warning. She was neither ready, nor was she inclined to take on this huge responsibility.

Brigette preferred to take charge of the overseas operations. It gave her reason to travel and be away from the head office and the late Saraswati's chamber, now occupied by Neha. It was Kiran who was now in charge of headquarters, assisting and guiding Neha. Ruzbeh had been deeply affected by the death of his close friend, and had become inert and apathetic to the business and Kiran had to do his share of the work as well. Sridhar emerged as the company's guardian and ensured hard work and loyalty for every penny paid to him by the company, working extremely hard to keep the company afloat in these difficult times.

Neha wondered how she could fill the space left by Saraswati. He had been almost larger than life, very renowned and respected, and had run the business so successfully that his loss had hit them hard. He had left a vacuum. Neha knew: Business is conducted through goodwill, experience and nurturing a network, and Saraswati had done that with élan. Neha was a novice and had a long way to go to fill up this void. How could she ever fit into his shoes? Would she ever be her father's daughter?

Neha never had the time to mourn her father's death. It had been sudden and now she was thrown into the deep end to run his business. There was too much action, too many developments, so much work to be done before she could have time to herself to remember her beloved father. And, the thought of Saraswati's death made her feel guilty—memories of her father and her misdemeanour bothered her. She held herself responsible for his death. She tried to cope with her guilt by drowning herself in work and keeping herself busy.

If that photograph hadn't come out, if her father had not been so deeply affected by it, if she had not stayed away, if she had come back earlier... there were so many ifs... and so many regrets. She would have to do something drastic, something unexpected, something out-of-the-box to stop feeling this overwhelming culpability and be at peace with herself. But for now, she was trapped in vicious remorse and regret. Her beloved father was no more. Not only was there an unfathomable ache within her, but also a darkening sense of repentance.

8

Rolled in Hot Furnaces—Steel

Even before Neha could take control and command of the responsibility and status bestowed on her, *Forbes* magazine celebrated her foray into her father's shoes. Neha was declared the richest woman in the world, and the most powerful female business leader. However, Neha was astonished not to find her place in the prime list of the rich and famous. They were all men; men of different nationalities, races and age. Truly, the world is not a place for women, she told herself. No women were on the list. It was the same sad narrative of patriarchal power, which had ruled the world, century after century. A bastion that women found difficult to penetrate.

What intrigued Neha was the photograph the magazine carried of her. It depicted her facing the camera in a sleek, sporty dress with a pink golfing cap, hitting a huge shot with a wood. The fallen tee, the ball rising with great speed and herself, bent in a perfect swing, created a dramatic effect. Neha did not recollect where and when it was shot, but she was overwhelmed. Neha had never seen herself look better than this.

Neha suddenly foresaw a challenge. A spurt of nirvana, bodhisattva, and ultimate realisation, something that seldom rushed in within a single moment. She had to make a place for herself in the principal list. She had to be at the top of the main list. This would be her tribute to her father. Her redemption and her narrative. She would lead the *Forbes* list, and very soon, for certain. That was her dream and her ambition—to storm that privileged male bastion.

Will power, determination, dreams and lofty aims alone do not make the recipe for success. To attain her goal, she had to create a conducive environment and have a well-founded strategy. A good team, a well-formulated project, patience, endurance and hard work had to be her ingredients. She had to move out of her comfort zone and reinvent herself in order to reach this pedestal. She needed to forge a new path.

Neha requested Sridhar to take over as managing director of the steel business and made Ruzbeh the acting chairman. She decided to take baby steps into the arena of wealth creation, with Kiran as her key associate. They toyed with ideas, projects and plans to achieve a place at the top of the league. They had deep pockets, so money was not a problem. And, they could create formidable teams. What she required was an idea that she could be passionate about... the rest would follow suit.

The next few months were devoted to determining the right area for business diversification. It required a lot of research and numerous site visits and interactions; they also needed a thorough understanding of the business and its potential competition, a clear vision and a sound blueprint. Kiran had arranged for several presentations on new business ideas and interfaces with bankers, consultants, start-ups, promotors, market analysers, economists, researchers, psychologists and statisticians.

First, they conducted an appraisal of the businesses of the companies already at the top. Financial services, banks, real estate, mining, infrastructure groups, pharmaceutical companies, web-based services, hotels, traders in bullion, fashion, apparel, franchise companies and many more had made it to the list of the richest of the rich.

In order to compete with them, it was essential to reinvent the business, have a unique strategy, innovate dynamically and produce technological progression. This was the plausible way to make a paramount difference. Presentations were made in varied areas, including investments in taxi aggregation services, home stays, web-based delivery of goods, entertainment platforms, breweries, search engines, social media platforms, internet telephony, blogging, vlogging, video conferencing, crypto-currency, artificial intelligence, block chains and the internet of things.

Neha understood that it was the advent of radio, followed by television, that had really changed the world after the printing press, railroads, electricity and motor cars. In recent times, it has been the world wide web and mobile technology that has completely transformed the way we live.

Thus Block chain, internet of things, artificial intelligence and robotics seemed promising. Similarly, bio-technology, bioinformatics, fuel substitutes, genetics, stem cell therapy and nano-medicine also held huge potential. Ultimately, to create a business of immense value and a gargantuan canvas, they needed to provide an affordable, sustained and effective solution for a universal problem. They could do this by introducing something new, something to make life easier and more meaningful for

people; additionally their concept also needed to augment joy, happiness and a sense of well-being. The proposal needed cross-border appeal, touching the lives of people across continents, countries, cities and even percolating down to the villages. The venture had to make people enthusiastic about the future and provide them with contentment and hope. It should be something that civilisation was simply waiting for to be placed on mankind's lap as a welcome package that cannot be discounted.

Electricity brought light and comfort to our homes. The radio brought news and entertainment. Telephony brought us closer and information technology created a seamless world. Neha realised that to be a world business leader, something as significant, something as revolutionary was required to be proposed. They had to do something that would prove to be a game-changer—something that would shake up the world and bring about drastic changes in people's lives while fulfilling an unmet need. She had many options.

Artificial Intelligence had already made a mark. It removed human bias from decision-making. Artificial Intelligence could reduce human-related errors, which caused a majority of road accidents or calamities. Mankind would no longer be wasting time in repetitive drudgery. Instead, people could put their energy to use in being creative. Interactive video conferencing platforms would make one connect from any location and reduce time wasted in travel. It would make online learning effective. Thousands of people meaninglessly confined in offices, judicial courts and prolonged meetings, would get a respite. Working from home would become a norm and teams could be created in moments. The value of time would further increase.

Block chains would integrate various mundane activities.

Regulatory compliances, paying of bills, checking documents, verifying, validating, referencing and cross-referencing would become easy. Further, cheating, scamming and hacking would become difficult. The world would become a safer place. Robots would perform precise tasks and remove the toil of cooking, washing, cleaning and decluttering, so as to make human life more worthy, more meaningful and devoid of senseless toil.

Crypto-currency would make us all global citizens. The hidden financial payoffs, banking surcharges, impact of monetary and fiscal policies, national taxation and economic subjugation would be vastly reduced. Individuals would gain freedom from national economic policies, and capital would have the capacity to fly to a more efficient regime. This would create pressure to reduce trade barriers and would induce the correct value for one's skills and labour. True capitalism and free trade would emerge, safeguarding mankind from economic imperialism.

Nanoparticles and stem cells provided a new arena for human health and rejuvenation. The potency and regenerative powers of stem cells could be safely used to treat somatic and non-somatic diseases, hitherto having no line of treatment. Nanoparticles would greatly reduce the side effects of current pharmaceutical formulations. Bioinformatics was also the future of human ingenuity.

Renewable energy and alternate sources of power have already taken the world by storm. Energy from the sun, sea waves, geothermal heat gradient, wind, biofuel and biomass could reduce the carbon footprints of fossil fuel, coal and other such conventional resources.

Neha visited all these laboratories, experimenting with painless meat through tissue culture, labs that increased food

production through hydroponics, making alternate food and fuel from algae, making equipment to improve sleep quality, for better bowel movement and to extend orgasms. She studied the use of nootropics to reduce stress, augment happiness, and increase energy levels. The human trials, efficacy and safety issues needed to be addressed and ironed out before their widespread use; this would require time. The uncertainties involved in such endeavours were enormous.

For months together, this process to discover the right business went on without any pause. Kiran would organise fresh sets of presentations, consultations, visits and interactions. Neha would stringently prepare before every meeting. She would try to learn as much as she could about the subject so as to be participative and ask intelligent questions. Many of the business models were complex and required effort to be grasped intuitively. Neha used her time very productively—working hard, burning the midnight oil, surfing the internet, referring to journals, exploring background material, going through texts and analysing the consultants' documents.

She didn't want a moment for herself, as that would remind her of Saraswati and his untimely death. She wanted to escape these thoughts and memories. She wanted to forget the fact that she was now an orphan, alone, without any emotional sanctuary. Hard work was her only refuge. Neha was convinced that her achievements alone would, probably, one day, provide her with a sense of sanity. She buried herself in her work, working harder and harder with no breaks. That was the only way to wash away her sorrow and loneliness.

The business plans presented to her had the potential to succeed. A good team and the investment of capital would ensure success in many of these ventures. Although she had no expertise and no experience whatsoever, she felt that these handicaps could be addressed. However, she was yet to feel connected to the ideas being presented. Money alone could not forge a successful business. At least not in her case.

Neha needed to be passionate towards a cause. She wanted a genuine reason for investing time and energy in a venture. It had to be something close to her heart. It needed to be about a real human issue that required an urgent solution. And then, Neha could provide a solution that was workable and saleable. She could lead the *Forbes* list by offering a panacea, something new, something ground-breaking... something that would make a difference, that would touch hearts and enhance lives, lifting people from the drudgery that defined it. She was determined that her solution would not be a copy of something else—it was not about repackaging something that was already in existence, not about mundane solutions. It needed to be brand new and innovative and definitive.

Kiran was now growing impatient and restless by what he perceived as Neha's slow response. He saw it as dithering. He was working hard and providing several options in terms of new businesses that Neha could explore. But nothing seemed to interest her. Her lack of enthusiasm was upsetting him.

And then, one fine day, Neha revealed the truth.

'People think that my father came to the steel business and metallurgy only to create wealth. He was an engineer trained in metallurgy. He saw a huge opportunity in steel. All of this is true, but there is a greater truth.'

It did not surprise Kiran.

After all Saraswati hailed from an under developed nation—

India, which still nursed its colonial hangover.

'A nation where people's entrepreneurship, their dreams and their initiatives were crushed. It was a nation that served as a source of raw material and a market for finished goods,' she sighed. 'A country denied manufacturing and building infrastructure. He knew that if India had to be built, steel would be the key raw material.'

If India needed bridges, roads, skyscrapers, airports, railways, metros and a huge manufacturing and service sector, it would need a huge amount of steel. The country would need steel to build automobiles, aircrafts, weaponry, efficient transport, housing for all, agricultural engineering, heavy machines, earth movers, designer goods, popular brands, textile, tourism, architecture and space crafts.

He would produce steel for all of this, Neha explained. Her father had a deep-seated desire to make steel affordable. He wanted to make steel surplus. He would make so much steel that it would percolate to underdeveloped countries and give them an opportunity to develop quickly. He would make the processes efficient and easily scalable. He would create a highly-skilled labour force and invest money in R&D and training. It was his dream to make developing countries self-sufficient so that they could forge their own path towards growth.

When Saraswati moved to Germany, Europe had not yet recovered from the devastating losses of the Second World War. The war had shattered the continent. The labour movement and unionism had crippled manufacturing. Government-owned companies were inefficient and were dens of corruption. Most of the foundries were closed permanently and others were on the verge of shutting down.

Saraswati saw a trend: an increase in demand. Europe was rebuilding itself. Private entrepreneurship was being promoted. Foreign capital was being welcomed. The Cold War had created its own requirements and the ownership of private cars, two-wheelers and other automobiles was on the rise. The old was giving way to the new. The city centres were being developed as business districts. All this was leading to a slow and steady increase in the demand for steel, which would surely see a much steeper rise in the near future.

Saraswati purchased an old foundry and turned it around to make it into a profit-making unit. He toiled hard, brought in efficiency and cost cutting measures, used migrant labour, improved logistics, found new variants, tried out new raw materials, diversified sourcing and ultimately, emerged successful. He was now receiving large orders and soon, he was acquiring bigger foundries and mills. Inspired by this success, Saraswati worked even harder. He created long-term agreements with bulk users, thereby increasing his order book manifold. Later, he aggressively forged a path to drive his business further along the road to success by buying many more defunct foundries all over Europe.

The emergence of the European Union provided him with major impetus. With a bigger market, easier movement of man and material and easier financing, Saraswati was now setting up his state-of-the-art steel mills all over Europe. He soon became the largest steel manufacturer in Europe.

At this stage, plants were set up close to the raw material sources, thereby giving him further advantages, including lower costs, and thereby increasing his lead. Soon, Saraswati Steels had steel plants all over the world. His company was now the

global leader in steel manufacturing. They made all grades and all kinds of steel, fulfilling the global demand for manufacturing and infrastructure building. All this happened in less than a decade. His hard work had paid off, and he had moved from one success to another.

Neha needed a similar inspiration, and a similar opportunity to put all of herself into a business. Only if she did that could she possibly be a leader and a winner, and ultimately reach the coveted place she was targeting. There was no room for compromise in this regard. Her father was her inspiration. He had started with nothing and created a global empire, climbing the ladder of success and never looking back. She wanted to emulate him. She wanted to be successful in her business—very, very successful. But she also wanted to give back to society, just like her father had. Whatever business she chose would have to make a difference, would have to touch people's lives and transform them.

Kiran was baffled by Neha's resolve, or rather lack of it, and was losing his patience with every passing day. He was tired of all the presentations and introductions to various businesses. Nothing seemed to interest her or satisfy her. How long could he and his team keep coming up with business options for Neha? He was left frustrated and unhappy.

Kiran respected Neha's vision. But he did not know where he could find a project befitting her calling? How did one proceed in that direction? All his efforts were of little consequence.

To Kiran, it seemed as if she was only doing it only as a learning exercise and to keep herself occupied. Other than that, this mega exercise seemed to be of no significance.

In the meanwhile, Neha had lost her grip on the steel business. She was totally engrossed in diversifying, finding her dream business. That was the only thing she concentrated on. The quarterly results for Saraswati Steels were heartening, mainly due to Sridhar's leadership and acumen. Brigette had spent days together at obscure locations to make the sluggish overseas foundries efficient and profitable, and to move them into a growth trajectory. The business was doing well, but it was not because of Neha, but in spite of her. And since Kiran had been drafted into helping her, he was losing his place in the sun—in the expanding business of steel, which was their real turf.

Before the first anniversary of Saraswati's death rolled around, things had stabilized. In fact, the empire created by him had become more formidable under the able leadership of his lieutenants, all except for his sole daughter.

Ruzbeh, the acting chairman, presided over the annual governing body meeting in the Berlin town hall. It was attended by thousands of shareholders. Once again, Saraswati was remembered and rich tributes were paid to him. After all, it was thanks to his vision, his hard work and his dedication that the empire had grown so big, providing sustenance, employment and so much more to so many across the world.

The yearly profits, turnover, valuation, new projects, and the financial ratios were all encouraging. A huge amount of dividend was paid to the shareholders after keeping aside sizable profit for expansion and new ventures. The share price of the company was skyrocketing, mostly due to the infrastructure boom that was sprawling in developing nations. Everything was hunky-dory as far as the company was concerned. But Neha was conspicuous in her absence. And Kiran was relegated to sitting in the visitor's arena, and not on the stage as he should have been, as a director. This was a terrible blow to him.

In the meanwhile, a business tycoon in China had suddenly disappeared, practically into thin air. A month later, a letter from him appeared, resigning from his position, which was hurriedly accepted by the board. Suddenly, one of his daughters stood tall and demanded his place, and authorities promptly accepted her as the legal heir of the tycoon. The board appointed her as the chairperson. The mystery daughter, Kim, was now the newly-minted richest woman in the world. More successful business women from China began to grace the papers, as the country's national policy promoted women to head some of the country's big businesses. On the other side of the world, a bitterly fought divorce made a U.S.-based multi-millionaire part with his wealth, making his wife one of the richest women in the world.

To add insult to injury, the *Forbes's* list did not feature Neha in the list of the richest women in the world that year. Her authority and position had been vastly eroded in the company, which she was heading only on paper. From being on top of the list—the richest woman—now she didn't even feature in the list anymore.

9

Tower of Silence

Before Neha and Kiran could take a call on their new venture to take the business to the next level, another tragedy shook their world. Ruzbeh was diagnosed with liver cancer. The eminent but ailing man had decided to go visit his ancestral house to celebrate Navroz, the Parsi New Year. Very often, when he was extremely sad and troubled, he would fly to Bombay seeking solace, no matter how brief, through an attachment to his roots. This somehow comforted him. To be back in the vibrant city of Bombay, cocooned within the warmth of his family, lifted him out of his blue moods.

After being dislodged from their homeland in Persia, the Parsi community, also known as Zoroastrians, took a long voyage to the coast of Gujarat. The local chieftain was wary about providing refuge to these people who hailed from a different culture, and who followed a different religion. Legend says that the chieftain showed them an urn full of milk, saying that there were already too many people and there was no space for more. Hearing this, the old Parsi priest added some jaggery to the urn, which dissolved into the milk without displacing the container or overflowing. The gesture worked and they were given refuge.

The Parsis kept their promise and lived in India, much like the sweetener dissolved in milk, adding value to the nation. They blended seamlessly into their new homeland, causing no trouble to their hosts, and all along, preserving their cultural and religious identity.

They excelled in many fields; be it business, manufacturing, classical dance, military, films, polo, dancing, photography, science, astrology, shipbuilding, aeronautics, as well as manufacturing the finest yarn and liquor. They had strong work ethics and had rather weird family names that depicted their trade—odd surnames like Jariwala, Daruwala, Canteenwala, Bhajiwala, Bandookwala, Lakkadwala, and so on. Strange names notwithstanding, they adapted to and adopted their new homeland with a fierce passion. They even fought against the British during India's freedom struggle.

However, over time, the community shrank, thanks to their rather strict laws on conversion and marriage. While this was done to preserve their unique culture in a foreign land, it had its negative effects. For men who marry out of the community, their children were brought up as Parsis. However, that was not the case for women who married outsiders. Men who married Parsi women could not convert to the faith. Over time, the vibrant community has dwindled alarmingly. Their civil laws had limited scope for conversion. For a Parsi woman marrying outside the religion would mean becoming an outcast, and soon the Parsis became an ageing, dying community.

Whenever Ruzbeh came to India he would stay in Colaba, a Parsi colony with beautiful, stately homes with common verandas and courtyards. He would meet his battery of cousins and older uncles and aunts, many of them unmarried, due to lack of suitable matches in the community. The visits to the various baghs, where the Parsis lived, the elegant women wearing ghada sarees, the ancient sculptures in the Parsi Panchayat library and above all, the fragrance of Parsi condiments and the distinct taste of Parsi food, brought Ruzbeh time and again to central Bombay, home to the largest conglomeration of Parsis in the world.

Ruzbeh routinely visited the fire temple when in Colaba. Fire was sacred to the Parsis and the *Agiyari* or fire temple was their sacred place of worship. Fire represents Ahura Mazda their supreme deity. Ruzbeh may have been away from his roots for years, but he had never forgotten them. They were an integral part of him, of his soul, of his very being. Visiting the fire temple brought him to his faith and to a great sense of inner peace.

When the cancer was detected, and his health deteriorated, Ruzbeh made a beeline for his beloved Bombay. This time, he had decided that he would stay put in the city among his family and community. He planned to return to Germany only if he recovered fully. Otherwise, he wanted to die among his loved ones and be sent to the next world in the traditional Parsi way, like his ancestors, where his body would lie in the Tower of Silence or Dakhma and vultures would pluck it clean. This ritual, for many outside the community, appears to be a brutal, thoughtless way to dispose off the dead; but not to Ruzbeh. According to Zoroastrian belief, the dead body is unclean, a potential pollutant and this is why it is placed in a tower and exposed to the sun and carrion birds. It is also considered the ultimate act of charity, providing sustenance to the birds with something that would otherwise have been destroyed.

For Ruzbeh, this trip was one fraught with pain. His cancer had spread and he was admitted in Bombay's renowned, Breach Candy Hospital. The doctors had done everything they could, but his cancer was in a terminal stage. There was nothing more they could do. They advised him to go home and spend the limited time he had left, with his loved ones.

Kiran flew to Bombay to be with his father during his last days. It broke his heart to see his father so frail and so ill. And what made it worse was knowing that he had so very little time left to spend with his father.

Ruzbeh had lost all his hair because of chemotherapy. This treatment brought a sudden autumn to a garden in full bloom. Once home, he wore a fateh, the Parsi cap, to cover his scalp and would sit in the veranda of his house, facing the garden with serenity. Now, he preferred wearing the dhugli, the Parsi traditional outfit and remained morose. Even in his frail state, he spent most of his time in the fire temple, reading scriptures and feeding wood to the fire, which had stayed burning from times immemorial. In the evening, he would watch the Parsi children playing in the garden. Later, he would demand a Parsi dish of his choice for dinner. Against his doctor's advice, he overindulged in food. He survived Navroz, the Parsi New Year. Ruzbeh jubilantly participated in the various celebrations. He feasted on the sumptuous festive food and provided handsome alms to the needy.

He also donated a huge amount to the Parsi Panchayat, which worked towards the upliftment of the Parsi community, and gave expensive gifts to the cousins who were looking after him. Soon after Navroz, Ruzbeh died peacefully in his sleep as all efforts to wake him up in the morning were wasted.

Now, it was time to bid farewell to him. Neha flew down to Bombay to be a part of the last rites of Saraswati's closest friend, Kiran's father and the acting chairman of her company. As per Parsi tradition, Ruzbeh's body would now lie in the Tower of Silence, to give back and provide sustenance to nature.

The Tower of Silence is situated in Malabar Hills in central Mumbai and is probably the most expensive piece of real estate in the entire country. Located in the heart of the chaotic city, in a 54-acre lush garden, it also breeds and grooms vultures.

Vultures were, at one time, a predominant species of large birds and were found all over the Indian subcontinent. They were a valuable resource in the ecosystem. Being carrion birds, the vultures ate dead animals. Dead cattle, dogs, goats and sheep would be eaten by flocks of vultures. They would pick the carcass free of all flesh, leaving only the brittle skeleton. Vultures are so efficient that an army could strip the carcass of a deer or a cow in less than thirty minutes. They played a very significant role in the ecology of a region by preventing the spread of epidemics due to decaying carcasses. When vultures ascended, villages, cities and roads would be clean. They were nature's scavengers. The advent of large swarms of vultures indicated the grim beginnings, of famine, death and decay and they were feared as harbingers of death.

Vultures are rather ugly birds. With their hunched stance, they look rather wizened, gnarled, revolting, and fearsome. And because of their association with death and decay, they are looked upon with repulsion. However, these birds save other species from communicable diseases, pandemics and contamination. Over the years, thanks to carelessness, indifference and greed, vultures had become a dying breed in India.

Vultures are intolerant to certain chemicals and hormones. Diclofenac, a medicine given to cattle to yield milk effortlessly, caused widespread deaths and the near extinction of this valuable bird. In India and Southeast Asia, the widespread use of diclofenac in cattle was linked to the deaths of millions of vultures that ate carcasses containing the drug. During the 1990s, this caused some of the vulture populations to decline by over ninety-nine percent. Diclofenac is lethal for vultures even in small doses due to the phenomenon of biomagnification. It causes kidney failure and then death as an effect of consuming the carcasses that have been treated with the drug. The Indian government banned the use of the drug later, but it was too late to save the vultures.

The spraying of DDT, a chemical pesticide, also turned out to be lethal. Unfortunately, due to this, the vulture population dwindled alarmingly. Soon, vultures were no longer naturally present in the ecosystem. They had to be bred and compelled to survive in an artificial, controlled environment to perform these rites. According to Parsi tradition, the dead were returned to nature as food for vultures as the ultimate act of charity.

As Ruzbeh was lowered into the Tower of Silence, the vultures were set free to eat his remains. Neha stood on a platform with his family and friends. She could see the swarm of vultures tearing the flesh off Ruzbeh's body with their sharp beaks, flapping their huge wings as they emerged from the tower after gorging on their meal. For Neha, it was something new and terrifying to watch the body of Ruzbeh being slowly consumed by the birds of prey. Neha was already numbed. Losing her father had been gut-wrenching and now, losing Ruzbeh, whom she considered as part of her family, came as a terrible blow. It was as if her sheltered world was collapsing, with her loved ones being snatched from her, one by one. The contours of her world were changing and shape-shifting, and she felt lost.

The sound of the flapping wings, the threads of flesh and blood in the beaks of the huge, ugly birds were already a fearful memory from Neha's childhood. Her terrifying encounter with vultures when she was a child was never forgotten and the memory of that awful day still lived on. She would often wake up in the dead of the night with nightmares of that awful sound. Drenched in sweat, shivering and sobbing, Neha would sit up in her warm bed, trying to calm herself. Now, after viewing this—someone she knew being devoured by vultures in front of her—she knew the nightmares were only going to get worse. It would be impossible to get a peaceful night's sleep. The vultures had returned to trouble her in a much more distressing way.

After a restless night, being continually woken up with the disturbing sight of Ruzbeh being devoured by the vultures, Neha decided to confront her demons head on.

Neha returned to the Tower the next day. This time, she went to the nursery where the vultures were kept. She saw their freshly-hatched eggs, the baby chicks, the mother bird providing heat and shelter to the young ones, their feeding, their nursing, the process of egg-laying and the males helping the females during the hatching process. It was the same cycle of creation, even for these terrible creatures.

Neha found herself a little less afraid. She took a few chicks in her hands and caressed them softly, watching as they closed their eyes in appreciation. Neha fed them with a swab of cotton dipped in milk. They had no issues existing alongside living creatures. The vultures only worked on the dead, as if it was their divine duty, their karma, their unique place in the food chain, their relentless service, their place in the canvas of life. They were there to cleanse the earth.

Neha slept well that night.

On her last visit to Bombay, Neha had been rather impressed by its vibrancy and charm. This time it was different. The sky was gloomy and overcast, pregnant with dark heavy clouds. It was the monsoon season and the entire city was inundated. In the densely populated areas of the city, water levels had risen rapidly and were touching the rooftops. A huge chunk of the population was living in relief camps, cars were left abandoned on roads as people got tired of spending hours together in their vehicles due to endless traffic jams. Hundreds of people had died due to drowning, electrocution and wall collapses.

However, the rains alone were not the cause of urban flooding. The inadequate and clogged drainage systems had a role to play. Urban planning had been a half-hearted affair; greedy builders had ignored the rules and occupied the low-lying areas, lakes, ponds, streams and marshes through dubious means. Land was precious in Mumbai and grabbing it was the easiest way to make a quick buck. By erecting buildings in forest areas and encroaching into the mangroves that protected the city, the builders along with an indifferent government had only made the situation worse for an already choked, overpopulated city.

Neha picked up *The Times of India* and out of habit, read the entire budget speech of the Mayor of Mumbai, who presided over the richest urban local body of India. A huge sum was earmarked for waste management, even though waste was all but encompassing the cityscape. Heaps of waste lay unsegregated and unattended; it was a common sight. The waste included biological, electronic and hazardous waste, and it made its way to the water bodies, streets, drainage systems and rivers, polluting every aspect of the environment. The vast amount of waste pushed into the sea, re-emerged on the coast during high tide, covering the beaches with filth.

If there was one thing omnipresent in Indian cities, it was waste. Human waste, animal waste, discarded packages, medical waste, dust, night soil, and waste emanating from settlements, factories, hospitals and slaughterhouses. The garbage, animal carcasses, glass, metal, plastics, chemicals and sewage were all mixed, making a deadly slurry. It was way beyond the competence and control of the administration. Barely any technology existed to get rid of this menace. The Earth was slowly becoming a planet covered with filth.

The limited free land available for landfills and compost yards, a vast amount of waste remained unattended, and was left to decay on its own. Much of it found its way back to nature. The sea and water bodies were already highly contaminated with biological and chemical demands beyond permissible limits.

Even in western and advanced countries, the scenario was no better. Although they had lower populations, their per capita waste and garbage generation was much higher. A huge amount of their waste was shipped to underdeveloped countries for recycling, and the rest was dumped into poorer neighbourhoods, making sure the gated colonies remain spick and span. In developed nations too, plastics, metals, sewerage, industrial and human waste posed a challenge. Cities around the globe were spending a greater proportion of their wealth to manage waste each year. And with rising populations, inefficient waste management and corruption, it seems as if humanity was fighting a losing battle, one that threatened to literally drown them into a sea of waste.

Neha was extremely troubled by what she saw in Mumbai. She was disturbed by the thought that in spite of having a huge budget for waste management, the city had squandered it or not utilised it. This prompted Neha to go down a rabbit hole, conducting further research on the subject. As Neha looked into it, she realised that it was a gigantic problem.

Waste was affecting every aspect of human life; health and well-being, aesthetics, beauty, the environment, the quality of water and food, the landscape! And the stench of garbage permeated the city's air; it was like a suffocating cloak that surrounded and encased the citizens, something one couldn't escape. The presence of garbage and waste around human settlements had greatly reduced the pleasure of living, the beauty of our habitat, and had made the earth an ugly planet to live on. It was all due to human beings and their eternal will to consume and consume more, with little thought for environmental degradation and the build-up of waste.

The local administrative units, cities, villages, countries, states and nations, were spending vast amounts on waste management and eco-restoration, in order to resolve all the related issues created by this mammoth quantity of waste.

That's when Neha had a eureka moment. After spending so many months trying to find a business idea that would align with her principles, she had finally discovered something. Waste management provided her with a unique business opportunity. A workable solution to this huge problem was warranted, and it was the need of the hour. Creating an enterprise around waste would satisfy her ambition, as well as her passion.

To implement it, she would need to be a vulture. She would break the waste down into its natural components and pass it back to Mother Nature. Neha would relish waste, feast on it, and make an empire around waste. Her excitement suddenly bubbled over. The last few months had been spent in a limbo—her father's death, then Ruzbeh's demise and her inability to channel her inner self—contributing to a sense of despondency. Now she felt energised again; there was vitality coursing through her veins. She had found her purpose, her goal. With her new business idea, she could channelise her passions and make a difference to the world—a positive difference that would contribute to the betterment of humanity.

She discussed the idea with Kiran and the very next day, he registered a new company and quickly got it patented. It was called 'The Vultures'.

10

Wealth from Waste

Neha and Kiran immersed themselves in research on waste management. For many months, they worked hard on developing models to create wealth from waste. They travelled together all over the world to check out various municipalities, landfills, incineration units and dumping sites to study best practices and promising technologies for waste reduction, waste segregation, waste collection, waste recycling and waste disposal.

In most local bodies in the underdeveloped countries, waste management was in its incipient stage. The unsegregated waste would be thrown into garbage bins. The local sanitary staff would collect this and dump it in a garbage yard. Kiran and Neha saw these dumps: they were an assault to the senses, stinking to high heavens, and the stench would overpower the neighbourhood. From the garbage yard, the accumulated waste would be picked up in lorries and transported to the outskirts of the city to a garbage dump. The garbage dumps stood like mountains, piled high with waste, making life hell for people living within a radius of a few miles. During the dry season, the waste would burn, releasing obnoxious gases, detrimental to the health of the people in the vicinity. The water in the entire region would get contaminated and the groundwater would not even be fit for any human activity, let alone drinking. At many places, the water and soil in the area would be unfit for agriculture too.

The garbage dumps also led to the creation of the dirtiest and most inhuman, undignified profession in the world—rag picking. A huge army of waste pickers, mostly children, and mainly girls, would descend like insects on the garbage heaps every morning. They would rifle through the stinking piles with their bare hands, often navigating the mounds barefooted because they had a better grip climbing the mountains of waste without shoes. They would sift through the rubbish and pick plastics, small pieces of metal, old furniture, old clothes, shoes, rubber, tyres, glass, syringes, wood and electronic waste like discarded computer screens and mobiles. They would collect all this and put it into their raggedly bags. They ate the expired packaged food and wore the discarded clothes that had found their way into the garbage heaps. Sometimes, they would get lucky and find something expensive—an old computer, a damaged cell phone, a decent pair of shoes, a broken piece of artificial jewellery, a disused watch, old sunglasses, mattresses, books and used toys. For them, the waste was like a treasure trove, full of things to be discovered and they embarked on their treasure hunt eagerly, indifferent to the stench of the polluted air that could damage their lungs or the shards of glass that could cut through flesh at the slightest impact. Grinding poverty made them unconcerned about all this. All they could do was burrow through the filth to salvage anything that would make their lives better, something

they could either use or sell.

In the evening, the waste would be segregated into a broad classification: paper, plastics, metal, glasses, clothes, wood, furniture, rubber, footwear, and then auctioned off to the recyclers. The rag picker in turn would get food, a place to rest and a meagre sum of money for their families.

To make matters worse, these dump yards were a beacon for criminals and teemed with illegal activities. They were sordid dens of crime, populated by paedophiles, rapists, drug peddlers, murderers, gangsters and thieves. The police found it difficult, if not impossible, to enter the dump yards to investigate a crime. It was a no-man's land, fiercely protected by the filth of human society as a place to carry out their nefarious activities. It was no place for law-abiding citizens, or even the enforcers of law. The huge mountains of waste camouflaged everything. Anything, including human dead bodies, could be hidden in these dumps. The all-encompassing, perpetual stink, the noxious fumes, and the dirt and filth, could conceal any human vagaries and the worst of crimes.

The recycling industry was full of holes. They were located in slums and in thickly populated areas in the hearts of cities. The useful material salvaged from the dumps would be cleaned, repaired, washed, stitched and resold to the poor. What was left was consolidated by heat, hammer and bare human hands. There were specialised workmen for breaking computers and televisions and for smelting syringes, metals and plastics. All this deconstruction took place next to butcher shops, tea stalls and eateries. The residences existed cheek by jowl with them.

The cities seemed to have succumbed to waste, with the majority of its people living under its toxic shadow.

In the Western world, waste management was better, but only by a margin. Most of the waste was segregated at its source. The colour-coded dustbins, higher levels of literacy and community leadership, ensured that glass, metal, food and paper did not get mixed. The recyclers also worked in a much more organised manner. However, landfills, garbage dumps and compost yards did exist and the stench from them permeated the air and polluted it. The people living in these neighbourhoods often protested about contamination, the foul stink and the spurt in diseases. To make matters worse, once waste dumps were established in a neighbourhood, the real estate prices would tumble down drastically, leaving the land to be further used up for dumping. Violent protests and demonstrations were likely thereafter.

A bigger menace was biological waste, e-waste and industrial waste. This was not only a nuisance, but it was dangerous to humans as well—used syringes were a health hazard as they could spread deadly disease, decaying bio-waste could lead to the spread of communicable diseases. E-waste had components that would contaminate the environment beyond redemption. The hazardous waste from industries could destroy habitats and damage ecosystems.

The normal landfills, protected landfills and incinerators could only add to a part of the problem instead of being a solution. A huge quantity of waste remained untreated and partially treated, even in advanced countries. Incineration did burn waste, but it also created air pollution. The landfills had a problem of leachates. The zero-discharge solution created a lethal powder, which needed to be secured and preserved under proper protection. There had been incidents of the concentrates being washed away during rain due to insecure storage, thereby causing a much bigger environmental problem.

There were some good practices for converting waste into energy, deriving fuel from plastics and rubber, using plastics waste as a component to lay roads, making artefacts from wasted metal and glasses, using bottles and cans as flower pots, recycling of metals, down-cycling of plastics and many more such innovations. In fact, many stores now only sold used and reused goods. Eco-friendly packaging was becoming increasingly popular as awareness about plastic and its dangers increased. Up-cycling and down-cycling were being embraced as well, since people realised that their environs were getting destroyed. But it was still only a small segment of the population that was environmentally aware.

Neha and Kiran visited universities, research and development labs and technology providers but found that they were of limited consequence. The technologies available were still in the development stage, and required a huge amount of funding to be able to proceed further in their research and provide a worthwhile solution. Then there were other problems. For instance, bio-degradation and conversion of waste into manure needed huge sprawls of lands. The logistics in transporting waste to compost yards was also expensive. Pyrolysis worked only on segregated waste. The technological solutions for waste management were at an incipient stage.

Many individual cities had made efforts to do something beyond the prescribed age-old ways. Pioneering work was done in certain municipalities for waste incineration, chemical treatment and segregation at source. The individual efforts were important but they were city-specific and location-specific, and thus they were not easy to replicate universally.

Waste was inert, Neha thought. More was needed to convert it into wealth than sheer technology, human will, financial resources and zeal. However, Neha was now passionate about waste and its management. She was consumed by her propulsion to turn waste into wealth. The vulture in her had become much more prominent than her business acumen. She had to solve this problem. For the sake of humanity and for herself primarily. She was willing to do it at any cost and face any consequences in her endeavour. Yes, she was determined and nothing was going to stop her.

Environmental jurisprudence and environmental law is based on the 'polluter pays' principle. Pollution per se is not a crime, but one has to pay for its management, and usually a minor fine for the offence committed is enough. Companies have to treat their waste through a process of anaerobic and aerobic systems before releasing sludge. The quantum of fine is based on the release of pollutants into the environment.

Thing were changing: the carbon credit regime was introduced to compensate for the loss or damage to the environment at one place by improving the environment at some other location. Planting trees, segregating waste, providing environmental education, eco-tourism and rejuvenation of water-bodies were some of the ways to earn carbon credits. In this way, the damage to the environment could be compensated. Lately, carbon credits have become a tradable commodity.

Although extracting wealth from the waste by sheer recycling was cumbersome and impractical, carbon credits provided a profitable business model. After extensive research into the topic, it was decided that The Vultures would generate carbon credits through scientific waste management, and then sell these credits to polluting companies.

One of the first companies to buy carbon credits from The Vultures was Saraswati Steel. The credits were generated by converting an erstwhile waste dump into a verdant urban forest by filling it with sand and earth and planting trees over it. However, this was a small dump that consisted primarily of municipal garbage. Also, it was a fairly limited challenge as Germany already had an extensive system of waste segregation at source and the recycling of plastics and metals. Thus, the garbage comprised household dust, organic matter and mostly materials that were easily decomposable. Nevertheless, thanks to her impressive know-how and meticulous research, Neha created a demonstrable best practice. Impressed and inspired by this, many more companies started trading carbon credits with The Vultures.

Nevertheless, the business was slow to take off in spite of Neha's concerted efforts. Neha realised that carbon credits alone would not make a substantial difference to her endeavours. It would take her decades to reach the position she wished to attain, which was the pinnacle of success. But now that Neha had found her calling, she had to move out of the shadows of being Saraswati's daughter and the heir to his business empire. She needed to stand on her own feet and forge her own identity. She wanted to be known for her achievements, and not as a rich heiress whose only claim to fame was her inheritance.

Sridhar was unnerved when Neha asked him to sell off forty-nine percent of her shares in Saraswati Steels. He had no desire to confront her about her decision. After all, it was her business now; she owned it, and he was just a caretaker, a loyal employee with no stakes. Once the real value of the shares was arrived at,

Neha hopped onto a flight to New Delhi. The influential Bombay boys arranged a meeting for her with the Prime Minister of India. The entire forty-nine percent of shares were placed at the disposal of the Steel Authority of India at par value, an offer which came almost as free.

Brigette, who held two percent of decisive shares, was now the chairperson of Saraswati Steels, and now, the Steel Authority of India became the largest steel producer in the world. They now also had the advantage of the latest technologies and the crème-de-la-crème of management skills.

The only thing Neha asked the Government of India in return was a policy of non-interference. On her part, the entire annual income from the shares held by her was pledged to a trust, which would provide opportunities for Indian students to study in the best universities around the world and provide seed capital to start-ups, thus creating prospects for many more Saraswatis. It would also give a chance towards the emergence of many more companies like Saraswati Steel. She wanted to encourage brilliant minds to forge the path towards entrepreneurship, and with her trust, she could help people who had vision but not necessarily the financial wherewithal to pursue their dreams, whether in academics or in entrepreneurship.

Neha's act was considered one of the greatest philanthropic gestures by any person of Indian origin towards the cause of industrialisation and progress. Saraswati was posthumously awarded a 'Bharat Ratna'– the greatest civilian honour in India. Curiosity about Saraswati and the company grew, and thanks to the media coverage about his meteoric rise and Neha's generous gesture, he became a household name. Now he was the true son of India, a country which he had left for lack of opportunities.

Neha was now free from the cage of guilt that had been shackling her since her father's death. She no longer felt weighed down by her privilege. She was no longer merely the girl born with a silver spoon in her mouth. She now had a purpose in life, something that elevated her, made her life more meaningful. The richness in her life was now derived from something deeper, something more than the mere trappings of outer wealth. Now it was inner richness that she craved.

Neha now found the freedom to be totally devoted to her passion. Being a vulture, seeing the world through the eyes of a vulture and cleaning up the world.

The Vultures were gradually emerging as a formidable player in the carbon credit market. Several companies purchased their credits to absolve themselves from their culpabilities towards the damage they caused to the environment. Many large multinationals gave The Vultures funds from money allocated to their corporate social responsibility coffers too, thereby funding The Vultures for their R&D, with which they could evolve new models for the recycling of waste. The Vultures became the repository of enormous experimentations in the field of waste management, research and development, as well as creating best practices in this field.

But none of these laurels brought Neha real wealth. At best, her company was a flag bearer in this field, but they were still not making any profits, neither were they close to emulating Saraswati's trail-blazing success in his business ventures. For Neha, who had grown up cocooned in wealth and privilege, this was a new life, a turning point defined by struggle, hard work and a drastic change in her carefree lifestyle. Nonetheless, she had no qualms about her life being turned upside down, about not being cushioned by wealth or being protected by her father anymore. She was out in the world alone, forging her own path... literally thrown to the vultures!

It is said that one's reputation can be one's biggest asset as well as one's biggest liability for companies as well as for individuals. Thankfully for Neha, it was the former. Her reputation and her lineage provided Neha with the opportunity to soon soar, right up to the big leagues.

She got an offer from a small French municipality. The city was on the verge of bankruptcy. They were spending more money on waste management than on education, health care and public amenities put together. Even after taking measures like cutting down on the staff strength, reduction in wages and a sharp cut in budgets for essential services, the local government was seriously short on funds. The presence of landfills and garbage dumps had reduced the real estate prices in the township. People wanted to leave the foul-smelling town and shift elsewhere. The city governance would soon be unviable, if a mass exodus ensued.

It was likely that they would become part of the list of ghost towns that dotted the country. This small town, once known for the finest wines, cheeses and chocolates, would soon lose its very existence and become history.

The Vultures signed a Memorandum of Understanding (MoU) with the city government to conduct a clean-up. The local government agreed to give fifty percent of their annual expenditure on waste management to The Vultures. In return, The Vultures would take full responsibility for sustained waste management and help bring the city back to its original glory. Neha had no idea about how she would achieve this unenviable task. She had no reliable technology or premeditated action plan in hand. The Vultures offered to take up the responsibility for cleaning up the town and restoring it to its earlier picturesque status. She asked for an eighteen-month gestation period to evolve the right strategy to take up the operations. And, thankfully for Neha, all her hard work and perseverance paid off.

From there on, The Vultures never looked back. Town after town, city after city, metropolis after metropolis were parting with a major portion of their budget to this company. It promised to absolve them and solve their problem of waste management. And, their successes were not limited to Europe. Even three large towns in North Korea signed MoUs with The Vultures.

Without any available technology, without any worthwhile strategy, without any real solution, The Vultures had received half of the budgetary allocation of most cities in their bank account. They went from success to success, colonising towns and cities, states and countries, and, finally, even continents. Over a few months, they became the richest company in the world... and Neha became the richest individual. Not only did Neha top the league of the rich, but she was richer than all of them put together. The sting of being removed from the *Forbes* list of richest women had now been erased. And, above all, she had also become the most powerful person in the world, with investments from almost all countries and most cities in the world.

The photograph on the cover of the magazine again surprised Neha. She was holding a tiny vulture chick in her hands and affectionately kissing it on its head. The photograph conveyed an emotion that was everything the Vultures stood for.

Being the first woman to lead the *Forbes* hall of fame, her spectacular rise in the arena of the wealthy made Neha a household name. She was discussed and debated in television shows, seminars, workshops and business schools as a torchbearer of out-of-the-box thinking, courage, endeavour, philanthropy and even beauty. Neha was now an icon. A position she had held earlier by accident and the privilege of her birth and not by any well-founded strategy or achievements of her own. But, this time, she had done it on her own.

Meanwhile, with clients aplenty and waiting, The Vultures were investing all their energy in finding a viable and sustainable solution. They had already been paid to undo the mammoth problem of waste that lay scattered in different locations of the world, threatening to drown the earth with its filth. Untreated waste in gigantic proportions piled and piled. Neha and her company were tasked with getting rid of it within a set timeframe. The money had been paid in advance.

Her team burnt midnight oil, putting plans and strategies in place for each city. Technological solutions were being evolved for each location, since each place needed a tailor-made solution. There was no one-size-fits-all here, there were so many variables. The pressure on The Vultures was steadily increasing. With each passing day, Neha's burden was heavier, and with that her stress. It was no walk in the park and there was no magic wand to get rid of the ever-increasing piles of garbage

In spite of her team working round the clock, and Neha burning the midnight oil to tackle the problem, the process took time and often, the results were uncertain. She realised that this was going to be an uphill task, one that needed constant attention and truckloads of patience. Each day, she would sit in her office, waiting for a breakthrough. This was all on her; The Vultures was her baby, her dream project, something she had invested her heart and soul in, and not just her money. It was something so close to her, something which was now a part of her. She felt raw, vulnerable and responsible for whatever outcome the company generated.

The Vultures were busy experimenting and researching. They were growing bacteria to eat inert waste, trying magnetic segregation of metals and attempting generation of electricity and production of fuel and fertiliser from waste. They attempted recycling waste, burning waste, composting it, deep filling it. Nevertheless, none of this was new. None of these solutions could solve the mega problem at hand. They seemed to be stuck in a quagmire, and it was consuming them, just like all those hillocks of waste were consuming the planet.

The Vultures seemed to be groaning under the weight of the very waste they were trying to get rid of. All of Neha's passion, desire, energy and efforts were being wasted. The wealth in the bank was fast eroding. The clock was ticking, and fast. The rollercoaster was speeding up and her clients were losing patience. Neha was facing the hubris of her ambitions, her guts and her folly. It was all too overwhelming. From the giddy pinnacles of success and fame to which she had ascended at a fiery pace, she once again felt lost, anchorless and orphaned. It was all threatening to tumble down once again.

Often, she felt like escaping. She longed to visit Jennifer and feel the warmth of embracing her best friend, whom she had known from childhood, who had been her inseparable companion, who brought back memories of happier, carefree days when innocence and fun had shaped their lives. She wished she could be a part of Jennifer's theatre group. Then she could act, or even help backstage. She could enjoy the hustle and bustle and creativity of the stage. She could just sit in the darkened auditorium and watch her friend strut about the stage. She could be part of the audience, watching in hushed anticipation. She could admire her friend, applaud her. Or maybe they could travel again... visit new places, soak in new vistas and cultures, try out new food... bask in the sheer pleasure of discovering new places, new mores, and new cuisines.

But she couldn't let this opportunity go by; she wouldn't get a second chance.

Jennifer, far away, was happy in her own world of theatre: busy learning lines, with rehearsals, performances and the thrill of applause. And there was more. She had found love. Her theatre director was in love with her. And when she wasn't busy with her demanding career, she spent all her spare time with her partner. There was now enough and more drama in her life. She had no place for Neha, and Neha felt deserted in her cocoon... Neha was alone, very alone. She had no one.

Kiran. But he was a colleague, not a friend. He was not one on whose shoulder she could cry on. He had never been there for Neha in that way.

Sridhar was of no help. This was not a business he was familiar with. Instead, he immersed himself in what he felt was the best solution during troubled times—looking at horoscopes and seeing what the stars had to say. He engrossed himself in her destiny and organised elaborate pujas for Neha's well-being at Vaitheeswaran Koil.

Everything seemed to be unravelling for Neha. The cities' authorities were raising concerns. The waste, which till now had inhabited outskirts and barren landfills, was now creeping into the cities and occupying prime space. The demurrage clause would soon come to haunt her. She had to find a way out soon.

Very soon...

Brigette was more practical. She advised Neha to remain focused and think big. Big problems seldom have easy, straightforward solutions. And smaller problems are often more intricate and complicated.

Moreover, all problems have solutions once we skilfully address them and are ready to apply ingenious solutions. Economy of scale is the biggest mantra for wealth creation. Even waste could be tackled by accumulating it on a bigger scale and filling up a larger canvas.

11

African Adventure

Neha sent a team to identify the biggest potential dump yard of the world. A few days of research confirmed that it was the sea.

The oceans and seas were historically the largest sink for the waste created by humankind. Even the nuclear waste from nuclear power plants, discarded weapons and nuclear arson were buried deep in its waters. A suggestion had been made that big cages be constructed and the waste generated by humanity be placed within them. As and when appropriate technology was developed, the waste could be re-extracted and treated. In addition, huge tanker ships capable of carrying tonnes of oil were now available as the world was shifting to alternate sources of energy, including nuclear energy, and even cars and aeroplanes were now running on electricity. The waste could be loaded on these ships and they could just float around, until a viable alternative was found.

However, this was not a permanent solution. Dumping waste in the sea came with its own set of dangers as well. The seas were already polluted. Humans had already degraded the land; now they were degrading the sea and putting all marine life in danger, threatening the rich biodiversity of the oceans. Marine litter and solid waste posed economic, environmental and aesthetic problems and also threatened human health.

Neha knew that a permanent technological solution could only be found on land. She needed a dump yard to create an economy of scale, where an appropriate technology could be tried and tested to find a permanent solution. She had to create a huge factory to deal with waste. First, she urgently needed to find an enormous vacant site to set up a laboratory and conduct her experiments with waste. They needed a country where environmental laws were not strict; it needed to be sparsely populated with large tracts of vacant, unused land available to them.

The democracies of the world with their own laws and complicated perspectives on environmental issues were unlikely to allow The Vultures to conduct experiments in their nations. It would invite too much controversy. Even a poor nation with a democratic government would baulk at the idea because they would need to convince their vote banks to permit the import of waste. It had to be an autocracy, a monarchy, where she could deal with one person alone—someone who could be decisive and in command. Yes, somewhere where a single man's word was law.

Central Africa was among the poorest regions of the world, and it was sparsely populated, with a low population density. People were either hunter-gatherers or were engaged in primitive agriculture. There were large deserts and dry tracks across the area—barren wastelands, where hardly anything grew. The trees had already been axed for building the railways. Imperial mining activities had left scars on the land, pockmarks that would wound the land forever. The abandoned mines, testimony to man's greed and indifference to the land that enriched him, had left deep pits. Colonial powers could never occupy and administer this difficult terrain. They had descended on the land, exploited its mineral wealth and stripped it off its natural wealth, and left.

It was only the monarchy that kept it alive as a nation state. The various tribes showed allegiance to the king, and he brought in the much-needed amity amongst them all. This was one of the most peaceful regions of Africa, headed by a monarch, a ceremonial army and no rigid systems of command and control. Laws were administered by the community and a barter economy flourished.

The King was the binding force of the country, and he managed to keep the nation together with a namesake currency, not-so-well-marked borders and a completely decentralised administration. The monarchy provided them with enough thread to weave the land into a country. The monarchy also occupied a very special place in the hearts of the people, in their culture and their folk tales. The king was omnipotent, even without being visible, and he was revered by his subjects. Fortunately, for them, he was a benign monarch, not a dreaded tyrant. It was an unusual monarchic system, something quite different from what people's perception of the monarchies were, around the world.

Neha had been in touch with the king of this Central African nation and he seemed interested in her proposal. His nation struggled under crippling poverty, drought and was perpetually ravaged by the greed of the erstwhile colonial masters. He was interested in exploring new ways to make his country rich, thereby giving his subjects a higher standard of living, lifting

them out of the grinding poverty that was their lot and giving them a better life. It was decided that Neha would fly to meet him with Kiran and two of her other associates in a small, chartered aircraft, which could land on the sole airstrip that the nation had.

On touching down at the tiny airstrip and going through what served as the airport—barely a few planes and a large yard—Neha and her team were chauffeured to the king's palace through the small city, which was the capital of the kingdom.

The capital city was more of a town, and had a few diplomatic offices, a central bank, a post office, railway station, government offices, and spacious bungalows for senior government officials. The paved city centre was modern—budget hotels, coffee shops and restaurants dotting the area. One part of the city was segregated as the cantonment area for the army regiments, while the other side was where the local citizens lived. Compared to the well-designed areas where the government officials and army folk lived in stately bungalows with neat lawns, the local area was congested. Its streets were narrow, next to cheek-by-jowl shanties, noisy bazaars and a stream of people perpetually flooding the roads. Driving a few miles out of the capital, it was rugged terrain, embracing quintessential African wilderness with miles and miles of savannah and blue-purple mountains in the distance.

Neha kept an eye out. The open-pit shallow mines and deep mines had very little activity ongoing as the miners had moved to mine elsewhere, leaving behind large pits, discarded mining equipment and towns where nobody lived. The country was home to many such ghost towns, she had read. They had earlier been prosperous centres, but now lay, abandoned and spooky.

The erstwhile colonial predators had built linear railways

running into hundreds of miles. In some pockets with water sources available, agriculture flourished. Other regions were either evergreen, semi-arid and arid jungles, surrounded by a vast desert, inhabited by nomads who lived in makeshift tents with their clan, camels and herds of cattle, goats, sheep and watch dogs. The tribes that inhabited the jungles thrived off the jungle, hunting and collecting minor forest produce.

As there were no good hotels in the city, Neha and her team were accommodated in the palace guesthouse; an annexure to the main building. She glanced at the main palace while driving to the guest house. It was a regal edifice, built in typical European style, with structures added on the ramparts over decades.

They drove in through a huge, majestic gateway. A long driveway, fringed by lush lawns, bordered by vibrant flowering bushes, took them to the palace. The massive structure was built of pink stone, capped by a central dome. Neha could see large, curtained windows and balconies looking out onto the luxuriant lawns.

King Ayola had personally ensured that Neha and her team were made comfortable. Neha was pleasantly surprised to see that an Indian cook had been specially hired to serve delicious vegetarian fare of her choice. Her living quarters were comfortable with modern amenities, something she had been a bit worried about. When she saw her bathroom fitted with a western-style toilet and a water closet, she heaved a sigh of relief. A copy of the local newspaper, translated in English, along with a few books on the history of the region, had been thoughtfully placed on the ornate table in her suite.

Neha quickly unpacked. She placed a photograph of Saraswati, Usha and herself as baby Neha on the bedside table. She always carried it with her, wherever she travelled. It gave her a sense of comfort, a feeling of never being too far away or lost. She also adorned the table with miniature figurines of Lord Ganesh, the Hindu God of Wisdom, and Lakshmi, the Goddess of Wealth, along with some incense sticks, a matchbox and a bell. She then pulled out her rudraksha beads, just in case she wished to chant, and thoughtlessly placed a large cushion on the floor, for her to sit cross-legged and meditate.

Neha wandered around her charming bedroom. The large French windows led out to a balcony. There was a sprawling golf course a stone's throw away. She stood there and soaked in the beauty of her surroundings, sighing with contentment as she breathed in the fresh air and looked out at the sea of green. Enthused by the sublime beauty of nature, she returned to the room and prepared herself for her meeting with the King. It was scheduled for the next morning.

Neha had been expecting a formal welcome for herself and her team, and had prepared to greet courtiers and senior officials. However, she was pleasantly surprised—and secretly thrilled—when she saw the King himself, standing there to greet her at the entrance to the palace, with just one uniformed guard next to him. He was tall and muscular; dressed in a well-tailored suit, yellow tie and oxford shoes. Standing there with a polite yet welcoming smile on his face, Neha thought he seemed quite unassuming—not haughty, aloof or arrogant like she would have expected royalty to be. In fact, she smiled to herself, thinking he could have easily passed for a well-groomed, well-mannered and agreeable World Bank executive. Neha felt an instant connection with him and felt very comfortable in his humble presence.

The palace was huge and rather imposing. The massive hall

that led into it gleamed with marble floors, its walls were covered with intricate wall art, beautiful antique furniture and tasteful artefacts from all over the world. Huge paintings of the king's ancestors adorned the corners of the palace, and seemed to stare down at Neha with regal splendour as she walked through the long corridor to the conference room. The conference hall, in contrast to the lavish décor of the palace, was rather minimal and modern, like any boardroom in a swank corporate office, only larger and maybe a tad more stylish. There was a large rosewood table in the centre. King Ayola and Neha pulled out chairs somewhere in the middle of the glass-topped table and sat, facing each other, with an equal number of representatives at their beck and call.

Kiran got up smartly and gave a detailed presentation on their proposal. The financial and technical experts joined him to explain the nitty-gritties. The Vultures would take over the kingdom for a period of twenty years on lease for waste management. Each citizen of the nation would be paid his cumulative earnings for this period of occupation in advance. Other than a very few jobs of expertise, the citizens of the nation would be first in line to be employed in the company's operations. The Vultures would also construct modern townships for the employees at various locations. The remaining families would have the choice to either live in resettlement colonies, or to leave the country. They would be paid compensation and rehabilitation costs. After twenty years, they would be free to return.

The Vultures had done their homework well. They had prepared a detailed map of the areas where the dumps would be cast and outlined locations for landfills, incineration plants, compost yards, research and development units and other

establishments. They knew the exact number of people they would need to employ and the number of those who would be displaced. They had detailed the costs for all these operations, civil works, equipment, capital, logistics and recurring costs. The Vultures offered the king retention of the capital city and a sizeable number of shares in the world's wealthiest company.

The king listened silently with a thoughtful expression on his face. The Vultures were making aggressive presentations in the boardroom. It was as if they had already taken over his kingdom. He never uttered a single word. His aides too sat, silent, listening intently. Occasionally and nervously, they would ask for clarifications. The Vultures had come well prepared for the meeting, they had all the facts and figures on their fingertips and they were never found tripping or at a loss of words. They took a brief break for lunch, which was a lavish affair hosted in the adjoining dining area, and then returned, concluding their presentations.

King Ayola asked Neha to join him for dinner. She was surprised and happy. She was keen to meet the king outside a professional setting. Of course, like any person in the face of royalty, she wondered what she would wear. She laughed to herself as she looked in the mirror in her massive room. Luckily, she had brought along a black dress; it was professional, but sexy without being vampish or too dressy. She accessorised with tiny diamond solitaires in her ears and slipped on a slim chain, on which hung a beautiful, dazzling solitaire locket. A swipe of kohl on her eyes and a light lipstick and a spritz of Chanel perfume... and she was ready to meet the King.

The dinner was surprisingly informal, held in the residential part of the palace. To Neha, this area seemed more enchanting with its fountains, lush gardens, a greenhouse to raise saplings, and a series of magnificent, plush rooms. The garden looked like it had been decorated with magic garlands of twinkling lights hanging from the trees and draped over the bushes.

The elegant dining room was dimly lit, and the molten golden light gave it an air of cosiness. The king was dressed casually, in a t-shirt and jeans and looked rather boyish. He seemed to be the only person living in this section of the palace, apart from his attendants.

During the entire evening and over a long sumptuous meal, Ayola did not speak a word about the business proposal. This was the time to get to know the business partner who was offering him this strange deal. The king had studied in a prestigious boarding school in Kodaikanal, in India, as a boy, where children from royal families of many countries from Asia and Africa studied. He seemed to know more about India than Neha herself did, and had friends from all over the country. Later, he had gone to Cambridge. However, his higher education had been cut short due to a personal tragedy. His parents died in a plane crash and he had to hurriedly rush back for a coronation and myriad duties.

Neha also met the only other survivor of the dynasty: an old, frail, elderly aunt of the King who confined herself to her room most of the time and had made a quick exception for Neha. She took care of running the household and the staff.

The dinner went by pleasantly, as each exchanged information about themselves. By the time they had finished the meal, the King already knew quite a lot about Neha: her past, her interests, the books she liked, her interest in travelling, golf and Bharatanatyam. Neha learned that the King firmly believed in social justice. She was impressed, and a little embarrassed, on realising that he was very well read too. He was greatly influenced by Mahatma Gandhi, Martin Luther King and Karl Marx. He lived a rather unpretentious life in spite of being a functional monarch. Other than his interests in golf, rugby and polo, he enjoyed good wine. Lately, he had become vegan. She wondered whether it was to keep a check on his waistline or because of a moral imperative.

The two parties conducted a couple of rounds of meetings in the subsequent days, discussing each and every aspect of the proposal. Every evening, Neha would find herself in the residential quarters of the palace again—enjoying long, languid evenings with King Ayola. She soon knew her way around the palace. The king would play the piano for her, his long fingers caressing the keys and playing Beethoven, Tchaikovsky and Mozart. She was awed to learn that he played the piano very skilfully, and with great soul. They spent hours together in his personal library, which had an enviable collection of books, discussing poetry, autobiographies and travelogues. They never talked business...

The city administrators around the world were meanwhile getting restless. Every day, Kiran would get reports of resolutions being floored to cancel the contracts with The Vultures. He hired a public relations company to keep the issues under control. The Vultures were putting up a brave front. With the help of their public relations company they were giving an impression that a permanent solution was around the corner. However, the crushing reality was that they were nowhere close to a viable solution. All their efforts, all that research, all the experimenting and they were still clutching at straws. Now all their hopes rested on being able to work in this African country, simply because land and resources were available here and they could conduct their experiments with no breach of confidentiality. But even this one solitary option was yet to be stamped, and deliberations were moving at a snail's pace.

Day after day, the two sides would meet routinely for a few hours. There would be a set of presentations, a few queries would be raised and the meeting would end inconclusively. They were nowhere near an understanding, forget about a deal. Even a rudimentary agreement could not be drafted. The Vultures' offer was not even being seriously deliberated upon.

In the midst of all this, King Ayola had scheduled his cross-country annual tour of the kingdom. Neha was not surprised when the king invited her to join him on the trip. They would be away from the capital for fifteen days. Kiran and the other executives decided to take a break and go on an African safari while the king and Neha travelled. There was no question of them returning to Europe. To do so without an agreement would have been suicidal for the company.

The King's convoy was to travel in the royal railway train, which had a series of plush carriages, or rather saloons, for the ministers and high-ranking officials. The king's saloon was state-of-the-art. It was luxurious, extravagantly so, and there were compartments for dining and sleeping and a special transparent bogey that served as a lounge, from where one could enjoy breathtaking views. The king had added a gymnasium and a library to the royal carriage. Neha was accommodated in one of the compartments normally reserved for the king's family. The train would take them into the deepest interiors of his kingdom—into the countryside and its rugged wilderness.

The tour programme had already been meticulously chalked out. They would cover longer distances during the night. During

the day, the train would halt at specific stations.

The King and the other dignitaries would travel to the interior villages and towns by road. They would travel in motor cars, and where the terrain was inhospitable and there were no roads, they would go on horseback. In a few places, even that was impossible, so they would have to trek through the jungle or mountainous terrain, on narrow paths, to meet his people. Although the King travelled for several days every year, he would return to a particular area only once in a decade. The subjects would come out in large numbers, excited to catch a glimpse of their monarch and be bestowed with his divine gaze. Each would bring an offering to be made to the king. Nobody carried any demands or grievances.

The King would inspect infrastructure projects across his land. He wanted to take his country forward, jettison it into prosperity. And for that, he needed to improve connectivity and boost development. He strongly believed in the power of education to uplift people, and desired to spread educational facilities to each and every corner of his kingdom. He also wanted to improve the state of health care in his country. But being a backward nation, and with a significant chunk of the population illiterate and poor, it was a huge challenge. Nevertheless, with the meagre funds that were available at his disposal, he was striving to establish schools and hospitals to improve the lot of his people.

The poor and impoverished subjects never complained. They were used to a life full of hardship... they probably even thought they were destined for it. Living in these remote, far-flung areas, having no communication with the outside world, they did not know any better. The concept of revolt, revolution and a new order were alien to them. Each tribe had its own laws and societal structures. The only thing common to them all was allegiance to the King.

Neha would spent all her time with Ayola. From the moment she woke up to the time she went to bed, they were together—eating, travelling and talking. They would sit in the transparent lounge for hours on end, gazing out at the spectacular African landscape and marvelling at the wilderness. Many times, they would spot wildlife. A herd of elephants moving gracefully with their cute calves in tow. A sleek leopard running swiftly alongside the train. Packs of jackals glaring at them from their hideout. Hundreds and thousands of deer would suddenly emerge at a distance. Neha was fascinated by the African countryside—the diversity of its landscape, the dense foliage and the sheer variety of its rich wildlife and flora was overwhelming. Even a dead tree supported a large number of species on its lifeless bark.

The jungle had its own sounds. The train would sometimes stop in the middle of nowhere, even at midnight at Ayola's insistence for them both to hear these sounds emerging out of the pitch darkness. Under the star-studded sky, with only silhouettes and sharp outlines defining the world outside, they would hear the trill of insects, the sudden roar of a lion or an elephant trumpeting somewhere, piercing the pin-drop silence with their primeval sounds. On other days, they stopped to see a riot of colour with multi-hued butterflies fluttering without a care in the world.

The rain would whoosh past still ponds and lakes where crocodiles would be lying, lazily sunning themselves, occasionally letting out roars which cracked open the silence. The waterbodies provided sustenance to all the inhabitants of the jungle;

a place for them to rejoice and rejuvenate.

When they were not soaking in the raw beauty of the African landscape, they would engage in deep conversation; they would discuss world leaders, geo-politics, poetry and music. For hours on end, they would discuss and argue about Freud, Marx, Hitler, Keats, Ramanujan, Einstein and Mandela. They would agree, disagree and, most often, reach a consensus. Neha was surprised at how comfortable she was in the company of a king. She had led a fairly sheltered existence and had not spent so much time with a man, not even with her father. To her dismay, the fifteen-day tour came to a close too soon.

All the while, the King remained worried. The king truly loved his country and had so many ambitious plans for it. He wanted to make his kingdom prosperous, modern and even democratic. How long could these people live in utter poverty under the yoke of backwardness? How long could they be denied the simple pleasures of life? How long could they live in ignorance? Why was this the case? Because they did not have the capital, the funds, to build a modern nation. Just because they were too few and too far! The king had a vision for his country and a surfeit of plans. However, to implement them, he needed financial resources. Now, thanks to The Vultures, there was a solution in sight. However, the problem was that the risks were too high. It was a Catch-22 situation.

Now that she had returned, other than the palace and some historic sites, the only attraction for Neha in the capital city was the golf course. Her room faced the emerald green course. Just looking out at the vast stretch of greenery around soothed her, restored her, rejuvenated her. There would be a lot of hustle-bustle in the mornings as the town's elite would emerge in foursomes with their caddies, making a beeline for the course. Ayola himself often started his day with a game of golf.

On one Sunday, Ayola invited Neha to play a round of golf. After a few practice shots in the driving range, they both registered their handicap, collected their scorecards and moved to the first hole, their caddies carrying the golf sets behind them. He told her that one of the abandoned, open pit mines had been transformed to create the golf course. It was undulating, with curves and contours. Tall trees lined the sides of the course, providing much-needed shade in the harsh African sun. The bushes and the woods that dotted the course created quite a few problems for any novice.

The King looked young, carefree and cheerful in his Bermuda shorts and golfing shirt, with a leather glove on one hand. She realised that, just like her, he was a leftie when it came to sports.

Neha crossed the half line in her first short. Unlike Neha, Ayola took a lot of time to set up his shot. He would flex his muscles, set the direction, feel the wind, make a few practice swings and only then would he hit. He almost reached the green using a wood. Neha felt she had already lost the hole. However, the king kept fiddling at the green and waited for Neha to catch up. It was rather deliberate, as he probably wanted Neha to win.

The king was now hitting a short drive from the tee, falling just behind Neha. The course was beautifully landscaped and well maintained. The obstacles had a natural feel to them, blending in seamlessly with the course.

At one of the short holes, Neha found that she had hit a hole in one. All the players came to congratulate her for this feat. A hole in one happens once in many lifetimes and one owes it to luck. Neha's day was made, and she was thrilled. She felt like a

young girl after a maiden attempt at cycling without any support. They completed the game with Neha winning it and the King just a shot behind. She knew that he had deliberately allowed her to win. She thought it was so sweet and considerate of him to do so and was deeply touched by this gesture. This man can make me happy, she thought to herself.

After finishing a long eighteen-hole game, they retired to the changing room. There was a special area for the royal family. Soon they found themselves in the sauna with only fluffy, luxuriant towels covering their tired bodies. They poured the water on the hot stones as the steam sizzled and enveloped them.

The air was charged with electricity in the warm, steam-infused room. There was no one but them. Neha and Ayola looked at each other, their eyes speaking the unspoken, and before they even knew what was happening, Neha fell into his arms as he softly kissed her. He slowly pulled off her towel and soon Neha and Ayola were making passionate love. It was inevitable. It had been in the air since the moment they met. The chemistry between them was so strong—their shared interests, their ease with each other and the strong physical attraction. For days... weeks... the sexual tension had been on the rise, and now, finally, they had succumbed to their desires.

After a long, leisurely session of lovemaking in the steamy room, they showered together. When they returned to the clubhouse, Neha's name was already written on the display board. Her hole-in-one feat had been highlighted in a list of luminaries. The only other name on the board was that of the king's mother!

That night, when Neha went to the king's quarters for dinner, her favourite white wine was already chilling in the ice bucket. Crackers, olives and her favourite blue cheese had been artistically arranged on the table. Scented candles gave the room a cosy glow, and the fragrance of vanilla and cinnamon wafted through the room. They enjoyed their candle-lit evening, gazing intensely at each other with love-filled eyes all evening.

The king told Neha that the English meaning of the name of his kingdom was paradise. Now his paradise was being offered to The Vultures. Saying this, he laughed aloud. He was in a great mood and continued to make a series of similar jokes in succession. They poured glass after glass of wine, and with each helping, they laughed and giggled even more. The king got up, pulled Neha towards him and led her to his bedroom, where he gently took off her clothes. They made love several times that night. No dinner was served!

Neha and the king spent many days and nights like this, wrapped in each other's embraces, smiling, cracking jokes, giggling and laughing loud. She was again carefree, surrounded by the warm glow of love, Neha felt safe, cared for and happy. It seemed as if life was magical and Neha was walking amidst clouds... until the day she received a handwritten note from the king. It was time to strike a deal.

Neha had been relaxing in her room that evening. The king had excused himself, saying he had some other commitments, so she was getting some time to herself after a long, long time. Suddenly there was a knock on the door. A liveried courtier handed her an envelope on a gleaming silver tray.

Curious, Neha thanked him and took the cream-coloured envelope, which had the king's letterhead embossed on it to her table, slit open the envelope and found a handwritten note from the king. Her eyes turned wide as she read it. Written

in a rather prosaic—one might even say business-like style, the letter stipulated three conditions. Neha would have to marry the king, she would try to have a child with him and during the resettlement, she, along with the king, would be the last to leave the kingdom. The king had in turn agreed to all the conditions laid down by The Vultures, striking down the stipulation mentioning the transfer of substantial shares of the company to him. Was this a proposal to marry or an agreement to do business? Neha contemplated this as she read the note time and again. She suddenly remembered the three conditions laid by her father when she wanted to travel independently and break free for some time. All men are the same, she thought. They try to bind women through conditions and very often fail miserably. Nonetheless, a broad smile blossomed upon her face

Neha was deeply in love with Ayola, and she knew that he loved her too. She fervently wanted him in her life. But this was so sudden and rather too straightforward. There were no pretensions, no emotional appeals, no beating around the bush. The note was short and to the point, but Neha knew very well that the king had spent hours of thought and preparation to draft it. Every culture has its own set of values and every treaty has repercussions, and the king had been extremely circumspect.

However, he was also very clear and forthright because he knew what he wanted for himself and for his citizens. He desired that his kingdom become a part of the economic progress proposed by The Vultures. It would lead to generation of employment, creation of wealth, exposure to technology and increased visibility. With this business, he held out hope for his subjects, hope that they would be presented with opportunities and would, therefore, be able to improve their lot. But all possible threats and his worries had to be addressed. The citizens also needed to be convinced and taken on board. After all, he was signing off his kingdom to make it the waste capital of the world, a sink for global waste, the largest dump yard of the world and a playfield for The Vultures.

Regarding Neha, the king was aware that for a woman raised in Europe, marriage was not a matter of life and death, it was not so sacrosanct and not necessarily a bond for life. This was why he wanted a contingent clause: A child. He believed that a baby would provide an unbreakable bond, a link that could not be snapped at will, which would pave the way for a permanent commitment. He needed Neha to give him an heir. Once married, he and Neha staying in the country until the end of the operation would shore the confidence of the people who were to be resettled. They could not tactically leave before the entire plan was put into place. The king could not flee and escape to another country after jeopardising his kingdom; he would be present and be in control of the new venture, that he had promised them. The refusal to take the company's shares was to reassure Neha of his complete faith in her. The king felt that financial commitments were no longer needed. He and Neha would be a family, and the king would automatically be a part of The Vultures.

Brigette was amused when Neha told her about the proposal. For her, it made no business sense and she wondered how Neha, a carefree spirit, born and brought up in Europe, would fit into the strictures and traditions of a royal family, that too within an alien culture. Jennifer too was not pleased. She was worried that her friend was thinking with her heart and eschewing reason. She wanted Neha to give the relationship some more time rather than accepting this hasty MoU. Sridhar was non-committal. Instead, he immersed himself in an array of yagyas for Neha's welfare at Vaitheeswaran Koil.

It was only Kiran who stood by her. He had been a witness to the burgeoning relationship between Neha and the king, and he knew that Neha was most certainly in love with the king. For the last many days they had been inseparable, and it was obvious to any observer that they were very happy together. Kiran also believed that the king's involvement with The Vultures would be beneficial. It would be a sound deal as the king was intelligent, respected and had friends in high places. Having him as a part of The Vultures would provide the company with added respectability and increase its reach. It would be a formidable partnership and a superb opportunity for The Vultures, one that would help them to overcome the unprecedented crisis being faced by the company. Once the king was on board, compliances would be easy to avail. They could start the operations quickly and confidently.

However, the challenge was not over. Logistics were yet to be figured out. The waste had to travel from all over the world to reach Central Africa. An extremely tricky problem that was certain to escalate in the near future...

Neha may have had some initial misgivings about marrying the king, but they were quickly put to rest. She knew she loved him with all her heart, and while she had found his handwritten note a bit strange and rather unromantic, she was clear that she wanted to share her life with him. Soon, the kingdom was in a flurry, happy and excited that their handsome, bachelor king was finally tying the knot.

Even though Neha and Ayola had wanted a simple wedding,

the plans for the ceremony kept getting more and more elaborate with each passing day. Neha had a small guest list, comprising Sridhar, Brigette, Kiran, Jennifer, a bunch of relatives from Hisar, as well as a few senior company executives. Ramlal and some other caretakers arrived in advance to assist her. The Bombay boys also accepted her invitation.

Royalty, on the other hand, has its own vast network and infinite protocols and traditions. The king had many relatives all over the globe. The guest list grew longer and the preparations more unmanageable as they tried to accommodate friends, relatives and people of significance. But the king's aunt was supervising the entire affair, from within the confines of her room and seemed to be doing it efficiently!

Despite the large guest list, the king and Neha were married in a rather modest and private ceremony, both wearing traditional African attire signifying the virility and fertility needed to have progeny. King Ayola wore a strap over his head, colourful feathers adorning it. Neha's head band was fluffy and of a deeper shade of red, worn over an intricately done up hair. Their necks were wound with seven layers of beads of all the colours of the rainbow. Their gowns were hewn from rough-looking jute cloth, stating their harmony with forces that fed mankind; trussed at the waist with snake skin leather, it indicated the powers of the cosmos inside the being held together. Both of them sported high-heeled footwear, spangled with silver stars foretelling the happiness that lay in path of their lives. Their make-up was sparse but colourful, stating how marriage could be bliss.

This was followed by a grand reception that was held in the vast palace lawns. The whole façade of the palace was intricately strung with multi-coloured lights, the trees and bushes were draped, while white tents and marquees dotted the lush lawns. A jazz band had been flown in from New Orleans and they played soulful music that wafted across the star-studded African sky. The surroundings were enchanting, with the twinkle of lights, an iridescent moon and millions of stars twinkling like diamonds. Neha wore a beautiful cream gown studded with pearls, custom-designed by Versace, while the king looked dapper in a tuxedo.

The buffet tables were laden with exotic fare from different countries. Well-heeled, wealthy people dressed in their luxurious best floated across the lawns, the tinkle of their laughter and conversation punctuating the air, while liveried waiters glided around, serving drinks and offering snacks. Some couples drifted to the wooden dance floor laid out on the lawn and moved to the music of the band. Neha, her hand tightly clasped in the king's, was happy beyond her wildest dreams. When she had her first dance with the king, she rested her head on his strong shoulder and sighed a deep sigh of undiluted joy.

But the wedding celebrations were not over. After the African wedding, the couple flew down to Chennai in India and from there they drove to Vaitheeswaran Koil for a traditional Indian wedding. Brigette and Sridhar stood in as parents for all the various rituals. Neha dressed up again, looking resplendent in a vermillion kanjeevaram sari with a rich border, decked in gold. The king was sporting enough to don a silk, gold-bordered vesti and a silk kurta. Neha was worried that the vesti would slip off, but Kiran came up with a marvellous idea, and they secured it fashionably with a belt!

To initiate the hawan, Neha and the king had to say their names, nakshatras and gotras. To the king's surprise, Sridhar had already got his nakshatra based on his date, time and place of his birth. Sridhar proudly gave his own gotra to King Ayola, by adopting him as his own son and making him a part of his Shaivite clan.

Neha became the King Ayola's Queen and wife after taking seven rounds around the holy fire, and the king fastening the sacred thread, thali, around her neck. From this day onwards, Neha would apply sindoor, a vermillion paste, in the parting of her hair to signify her status as a married woman.

The wedding ceremony was followed by a sumptuous vegetarian South Indian feast. Having studied in India during his childhood days, the king was quite comfortable eating with his fingers and was not curious or puzzled at the prospect of eating off a plantain leaf. Sridhar felt that the couple needed to shore up their luck, and so, he took them to all the adjoining Navagraha temples to receive the blessings from the planets of destiny.

The visit to India was their first as a royal couple. Neha was already a household name and the press covered every single detail of their visit. Her marriage became a leading event in the papers. People wondered if India also could have their royal families revived to invoke such glamour, tradition and lineage.

Even though theirs was a private visit, protocols had to be followed. Both the Prime Minister and the President hosted a reception in their honour. After a full month of hectic activities and whirlwind touring, it was time to go back to Africa to perform their duties as a royal couple and partners in business.

Meanwhile, the first consignment of waste had arrived. It had taken a long journey. First, it had been loaded onto trucks to bring it to the railhead, and then dumped on trains to be transported to the port. The consignment was then shipped to

Africa from the European ports. Here, both the railways and trucks were used to dump it into an old quarry, which had been marked as the first dump yard.

The logistics worried Kiran. It was not viable. Bringing all this waste was costly and needed a huge amount of paperwork. The compliance regulations during its long journey also warranted elaborate bureaucratic interactions and significant documentation.

Very soon, more and more waste kept coming in, and large-scale dump yards were established, lining the railway tracks. The picturesque rail journey in the kingdom, which had earlier offered panoramic views of the stunning African countryside and jungles, was now history. Instead, ugly mountains of waste pierced the skyline on both sides, overwhelming the wilderness and its serenity, while the stench of rotting garbage permeated the pristine country air.

12

The Waste Factory

Now that The Vultures had found a global dump yard for waste and a playfield to leisurely deal with it, the next challenge was transporting millions of tons of waste being generated in the towns and the cities that they had partnered with. These were spread all over the world and the waste would have to be transported by ship, rail and road, which was time consuming and expensive.

However, this model of dealing with waste from urban habitations had sparked a lot of interest in The Vultures again, and the world was watching the process of transfer of waste with a great deal of concern and curiosity. The icing on the cake was the positive effect on their bottom line as their share values rose. More and more city authorities were signing MoU's with them, thereby increasing the company's net worth.

Various authorities were glad that their problems were being solved. They couldn't care less about what happened to the waste once it was moved out of their backyard. All they cared about was getting rid of it so that their towns and cities were spruced up and cleansed of the stench of their own garbage.

The kingdom was no longer fit for human habitation. The water sources were getting contaminated. A grey smog engulfed the horizon with polluted air. The waste fires often spread to villages, forcing the evacuation of the entire village and livestock. A perpetual foul smell of fermenting organic waste made it difficult to breathe. In the meantime, The Vultures were bringing in more and more waste, filling every available locale.

The Vultures had created mountains of segregated waste in the central African nation. Brigette had put up a rolling mill for converting metal waste into steel, thus solving one of their problems. The plastic waste was being moulded into furniture, and would be supplied to schools and hospitals in underdeveloped countries. For workers, they had set up townships with all the essential facilities, this included residential layouts with neat rows of houses, tree-lined roads, schools, hospitals, playgrounds and other facilities. The people living in the areas where mountains of dump had been set up were resettled in other areas.

There was only one occupation in the country now and that was waste management. Anyone not involved in this enterprise had to move. Neha and her husband toured the country extensively, trying to convince people to migrate as per plan.

There is no end to human endeavour. The Vultures wanted to work on efficient logistics. The entire IT revolution was made possible due to fibre optic cable networks laid across the globe. Today, we have fibre cables crossing continents and oceans to provide high speed connectivity. Rail and road networks have made it possible to transport goods to people's doorsteps. Satellites and mobile towers carry voice packets across thousands of miles with almost zero time-lag. Crude oil is transported across countries and continents through a maze of pipelines. The Vultures too needed an efficient system whereby the journey of waste from the point of generation to that of storage and recycling was reduced and optimised at a similar scale.

If they acquired a dedicated waste pipeline, it could be a game changer. Already, the oil pipelines were falling into disuse due to a shift towards renewable energy and hybrid cars. The nature of fuel was changing as storage and transmission of electricity was becoming cheaper. Experiments were even conducted to transfer electricity without the aid of transmission lines. The Vultures built the largest pipeline network in the world, integrating it into the existing oil pipeline system, and commissioned it within a surprisingly short time. Now, the movement of waste was seamless.

The city municipalities could thrust all the waste generated by them into a pipeline and it would reach Central Africa through a gradient in a matter of hours. There was hardly any recurring cost. Within a few weeks of use, the cities of the world became clean. Waste dumps, incineration plants and landfills became a thing of the past. All waste was transferred and became somebody else's problem. Now cities, towns and even entire countries, were restored to their pristine glory, free from pollution, from garbage and the stench of rot.

However, everything comes with a price tag. A beautiful country in Central Africa, which had been a paradise with clean air, teeming wildlife, a wealth of flora and fauna, had now become the sullied dumping ground of global waste, destroying its primeval environment and making it the most malodorous place in the world. Now, the Vultures needed to work on a solution to this new, looming problem. But that was proving to be a challenge. With the entire country piled high with mountains of putrid waste, keeping it clean and stench-free seemed almost impossible...

The Vultures were, however, on a roll. They were using every viable technology available to treat and recycle waste. Their partnerships and sponsorships to leading technical institutes and universities were bearing fruit. Segregated waste was now so much easier to manage. Saraswati Steel was the first to establish a smelting unit close to the waste dumps. Taking the lead from Saraswati Steel, a large number of metal companies, foundries and smelters, had set up units and were converting waste metal into steel, copper wire and other useful materials. One of the factories was even extracting gold, silver and other precious metals from discarded electronic circuits!

The Vultures had positioned themselves firmly in the recycling market. They had delved into it head on, fuelled by Neha's passion and now, recycling had not only become a lucrative business opportunity, but had also become fashionable!

Everyone was recycling old clothes, shoes and furniture. Units were set up to repair and polish old pieces of furniture and household items. Clothes, shoes and other personal items were also being washed, stitched and patched to be made as good as new. Their embroidery units added value to old discarded clothes. Once the clothes were washed and repaired, they were embellished with exquisite embroidery to enhance the outfits, making them contemporary and fashionable. A leather unit was set up for recycling leather belts, jackets, shoes, bags and purses. Now, thanks to The Vultures, a significant number of people had found employment in these units.

In fact, The Vultures were instrumental in reshaping economies of many nations for the better, generating employment and setting up factories, thereby increasing their Gross Domestic Product.

Neha and her team had roped in some of the world's leading designers to recycle and refurbish these discarded items. The Vultures established huge stores in posh localities and leading commercial streets all over the world, matching the scales of Ikea and Messy, in order to sell fashionable recycled goods. The stores became fashion meccas with the well-heeled and the youth making a beeline to buy environment-friendly, chic items. Suddenly, second-hand goods were not looked down upon; they were much sought after!

The pursuit of repairing, repackaging and value adding, the setting up of retail stores, warehouses and the sheer logistical challenge of transferring them to all corners of the globe where they would be consumed, was taken up aggressively. At this point, they weren't paying attention to the bottom line; profit was not the immediate goal. What they needed was visibility and awareness about their work.

And their strategy paid off.

The Vultures soon soared to fame, becoming the most talked about global company. They had hired the best marketing and advertising firms to generate interest in their products. With smart marketing and PR, they had managed to make recycling a fashionable word. It had now become a style statement to buy used goods recycled by The Vultures. Celebrities jumped onto the recycling bandwagon and sported recycled goods with The Vultures' logo, flaunting them proudly in public. This had a trickle-down effect—more and more people were clamouring for The Vultures' recycled goods. Now, even world leaders followed suit. After all, they had to portray themselves as responsible citizens, as people who cared for the environment and wanted to protect it from degradation.

Thanks to their innovations, a circular economy for many goods emerged. However, this came with its own set of problems. The circular economy had its own costs, wastages and unwarranted needs for transport back and forth, which meant that there were still costs to the environment. The additive pollution was posing a challenge for Neha. They would need to work around it and find a solution soon.

However, on the positive side, The Vultures were able to inculcate behavioural changes globally; by making more and more people now hankered for recycled products for their personal and household use with a sense of pride. They had created awareness about environmental degradation and the dangers it posed to humanity and the planet. They had made the 'three R's'—Reduce, Reuse and Recycle—a household term. And people were doing their best to incorporate these environment-friendly practices into their lives. For now, old was gold!

In the meanwhile, King Ayola was preparing a blueprint for the country of his dreams; the prosperous, modern nation that he had always envisaged. His kingdom was now an empty canvas ready to be painted with colours of his liking. It was to become a country with towns, cities, villages, agricultural zones, forests and plantations, roads, railways and airports, planned on paper. City planners were designing modular cityscapes that would come up on the vast tracts of soon-to-be empty land in the country. Minute details for residential areas, facades of buildings, schools, public transport, stadia, drainage, city centres, business districts, colleges, universities, auditoriums, malls and cinema halls were being drafted on potential maps with colourful symbols. The king wanted to transform his country—take it forward from the backwardness it had been steeped in—and leap into the 21st century. When his people returned, he wanted them to be awestruck and happy on seeing the new, gleaming structures dotting their land.

As a first step, a network of eight-lane highways and arterial roads were built across the nation. Most of the plastic wastage was moulded to lay the roads that ran thousands of kilometres. A refinery was set up to convert high calorific waste into fuel. The construction waste from demolished buildings in developed nations could now be used to reconstruct the cities in its hinterlands.

The world and mankind were finally at peace with themselves.

It had found a solution for its biggest folly—generation of waste and environmental degradation. Clean cities, the absence of the overpowering stench of rotting garbage and the sordid sight of waste in developed countries, reduced pollution, was a testimony to the sterling work of The Vultures. With persistence, hard work and innovation, they had solved one of humanity's biggest problems while also changing the way people consumed. There was hardly any city worth its salt or any significant human habitation that had not partnered with The Vultures. It was a win-win situation for all. The company, on the other hand, was the biggest beneficiary of the MoUs, the carbon credit regime and a world transforming into a circular economy.

Neha and King Ayola had become ambassadors of the emerging circular economy and sustainable waste management regime. They were much sought after, being invited to various international conferences to deliver lectures on environmental issues. They would visit far-flung towns and cities to forge partnerships and renew contracts. Huge posters of the couple would be erected whenever they inaugurated their mega stores for recycled goods. Not only were they in receipt of huge funds from the MoUs, but a large number of companies were trading carbon credits with them too. For many companies, it became a matter of pride and honour to park their entire corporate social responsibility budget with The Vultures. The Vultures had more capital infused into their corporation than the GDP of many nations. Neha and King Ayola had become a power couple, the most visible royal twosome, and their popularity matched that of powerful heads of states and world leaders. They were the wealthiest, most influential and most loved leaders of the world.

In the midst of all this hustle-bustle, Neha realised that she had missed her periods twice in a row. It was not long before an ultrasound confirmed that she was pregnant. She and the king were delighted. He would have an heir to the throne, and Neha, surprisingly also looked forward to motherhood, even though she knew that it would come with its own set of challenges. With her busy schedule, she knew balancing work and motherhood would be tough. But she had overcome so many challenges before. She would yet again cross the bridge when she came to it.

King Ayola wanted Neha to move to Europe to deliver as his kingdom had only rudimentary medical facilities. Neha, however, resisted. She was reluctant to leave the palace. It was somewhat an extended condition, added to the three conditions of her partnership with her beloved husband, Ayola. The heir to the throne and their child would be born in the fatherland. That was something she dearly wanted, and she knew that deep down, the king too desired the same. As a result, the king hired top-notch doctors and nurses, and upgraded the medical facilities of the hospital in the capital city to take care of any eventuality.

In the meanwhile, Nobel Prizes for the year were announced and Neha was conferred the Nobel Prize for Peace for her contribution to global environment. It was a proud moment for Neha, the King and The Vultures. All their hard work and effort had been recognised, and she was to be a recipient of one of the most prestigious awards on the planet. The Norwegian authorities had to make several adjustments in protocol, as it was the first time that the Nobel Prize was being awarded by the Norwegian king to another member of a royal family, a queen !

Neha received the prize attired in a loose African dress, trying to conceal her baby bump; the news of her pregnancy was not yet public. The king accompanied her. Neha sat in the front, along with luminaries from across the globe—men and women with the sharpest intellects and brightest brains. In the citation and declaration calling her to take the stage, her connection with Asia, Europe and Africa was highlighted. Her contribution to clean environment practices was lauded.

Neha gave a short acceptance speech, talking about her various encounters with vultures, the scavenger birds, and how they had inspired her business trajectory. She talked about the synergy of economy and ecology. About how business and environment need not always be at loggerheads.

She spoke passionately from the heart, 'Wealth can be created by working on environmental issues while healing the earth. Markets have made mankind move in tandem and be unidirectional. Now the time has come for a sustainable circular economy. All the world leaders need to steer their economies in a way that the environment is not adversely impacted, making life everywhere a matter of joy on the planet. The producers and the consumers, the developed and the underdeveloped, the rich and the poor, and finally, the strong and the weak, need to make adjustments in favour of providing opportunities to live a fulfilling life in a conducive environment. Historically, the world has fought for parcels of territory and slices of land but now, the time has come to collaborate and revive each and every habitat. We must revive instead of further exploiting a dying ecosystem.'

Neha's impassioned speech was received with a standing ovation. The global press couldn't stop discussing it in their op-ed pages. However, what made bigger news and headlines was talk of her probable pregnancy. Photographs highlighted her baby bump. Even at an event as significant and serious as the Nobel Prize awards, the paparazzi and a tabloid audience had made their presence felt.

13

A Paradise Reneged

The Vultures were scaling new heights with every passing day, and now, they were at the top of their game. The scale of their operations, turnover, profits, prices of shares, payment of dividends, their appeal and sweeping reach had brought them to a unique status. No other company in recent history had been so successful and so relevant. Their growth was phenomenal. Economists across the globe were in awe of their business model and sang praises of the organisation. The cities that had engaged The Vultures had rid themselves of waste at half the original budget and had, therefore, amassed significant money in their coffers for providing other amenities and infrastructure.

The emergence of a circular economy was being cited as a victory for the entire human race. Neha and King Ayola were much-loved and hugely popular ambassadors of this profound and unique business model. They were hailed as pioneers of a new movement—one that would help the earth reclaim its resources. They lent visibility, trust, glamour and a strong brand image for The Vultures.

In the meanwhile, Neha had delivered a baby boy, an heir to the throne. She had opted for a natural delivery and the baby was born in the royal palace. Two of the three conditions had been fulfilled with ease and success. Neha and the king felt blessed. Theirs was a fairy tale marriage. Not only was everything going along swimmingly, but in fact, things were going much better than they had ever planned or envisaged. Their marriage was flourishing, they had a healthy baby boy who was heir to the kingdom, their business was booming, Neha's dreams had come true, the king's country was developing rapidly, their personal wealth and that of the kingdom had increased in leaps and bounds, and Neha and King Ayola had become the ultimate couple—brand ambassadors for sustainable living, loved and revered the world over.

But, as they say, nothing good lasts forever...

On the surface, everything seemed to be flourishing, but the situation on the ground was not as promising. Now that the cities and consumers had been absolved with the responsibilities of managing their own waste, more and more of it was being generated and transferred to the kingdom, which had now become the world's sole dump yard.

Even though The Vultures continuously augmented their recycling capacities with state-of-the-art infrastructure, the volume of waste was enormous, and it had effectively converted the entire country into a huge waste dump.

Adding to this catastrophe, people elsewhere were becoming increasingly irresponsible, because they believed that waste and garbage were no longer their responsibility, it was someone else's headache. So, waste segregation at source had almost stopped. Consignments mostly came into the kingdom as mixed waste, and the employees of The Vultures had to painstakingly segregate it at the sink, adding to their already exhaustive list of functions.

Ashes deposited in the incinerator were to be stored permanently in secured landfills. The Vultures tried new processes: carbon sequestration for the polluting gases and carbon dioxide emitting from the recycling industries. It was an energy intensive process. The electricity production for this purpose created pollution at the site of generation. A compost yard prepared for cultivating organic coco had to be discarded due to the high levels of lead and heavy metals.

One of the consignments of waste had arrived, brimmed with old and damaged mercury thermometers, which had leached into the soil and the water. The Vultures had to pay through their nose for the redemption process to restore the ill effects caused due to mercury contamination. All the sources of water supply from the region had to be abandoned for several years to prevent mercury poisoning.

Those were not the only problems The Vultures were facing. Their unprecedented popularity, spectacular rise, publicity and hype that followed in their wake, had led to envy and anger amongst many organisations. While on one hand, they had scores of well-wishers, on the other hand an undercurrent of hidden enmity was also slowly building.

Other than that, some environment organisations had come together to form pressure groups and were demanding a thorough investigation into the strategies of The Vultures. In some European cities, nude protestors thronged the streets in the nude to rally against the company. They called The Vultures predators and accused them of having no clear-cut solutions.

Conspiracy theories were floated that Neha had seduced and then emotionally blackmailed the unwitting king of a poor African nation and converted his entire nation into a giant dump yard.

To make matters worse, certain weapons and explosives had been ferried as metal waste. As they were not segregated, they got mixed up in the smelters, causing an explosion in one of the foundries. The explosions caused the death of a few labourers and injuries to many, raising concerns about industrial safety during recycling operations. The media splashed the case across the world, making it headline news. Activists convinced the workers to sue the company. Finally, the case was closed; they had wrangled and managed a huge out-of-court settlement, which had drained the company's coffers. The Vultures were under pressure from civil society groups and environmental organisations. After this incident, things came to a head, with even the United Nations got involved. There was a discussion at the UN on the sustainability of such operations and the ethics of exploiting a sovereign country and making it a dump yard for waste, owing to a skewed agreement.

Just as she had once been feted and welcomed by the media, Neha now became an object of contempt and ridicule. It began with cartoons depicting Neha as a witch and King Ayola as her unwitting victim. One of the articles compared him to Nicholas II, the last Czar of Russia and Neha to Queen Alexandra, his wife who hailed from Germany and who was often seen as the reason for all his follies, and the collapse of Russia. From being a media darling, the tables now turned on Neha. She was starting to be hated, ridiculed and reviled.

She had been knocked off her pedestal by a hostile media,

worried governments and an anxious UN. The plight of the inhabitants of her new nation was now coming into question.

Even while a storm was raging around The Vultures, and their business model was being challenged, Neha and King Ayola were enjoying the joys of parenthood. They were absorbed in the daily minutiae surrounding the little prince, who was the apple of their eye. They would cherish his laughter, his first spoken word, his crawling on all fours, standing on two legs, the first time he walked and ran... every milestone was greeted with pride and joy. And they also enjoyed his yelling, laughing, crying for mundane reasons, and his joyous shouts. The prince kept them busy. They hardly had any time to even sleep or make love, so absorbed were they in their little heir. The prince had become the centre of their world, and most of their time was spent in feeding him, playing with him and putting him to sleep. All the humdrum chores that came with parenthood were embraced with enthusiasm, love and utter bliss.

As the prince grew, he started making countless demands. He insisted on changing his outfits several times a day. He continually wanted better teachers, and they had the best home tutors flown in from across the globe who taught him the three Rs. A tiny golf set was procured so that he could learn the basics of golf at a young age; the little boy would enthusiastically hit the balls in random directions. The king even got him a cuddly Labrador retriever puppy, who became his constant companion and best friend.

So absorbed was the king in pandering to and taking care of his son, that his administrative duties took a backseat. He began to postpone many of his tours and delegate a chunk of his work and administrative duties to his top-level courtiers.

Neha, too, was equally absorbed in her son, and work was no longer her priority. It was Kiran who shouldered the burden of The Vultures' work as Neha was engaged otherwise.

Neha had a weird dream one night. She saw a vast field, filled with hundreds of dead vultures, piled one over the other. After she woke up, she turned to her husband and told him about the sad dream. But after that first night, the dreams would not stop. Neha would dream of vultures, huge birds crying for help with loud shrieks every night. They were hungry, thirsty and dying in pain, in hordes. She would see lifeless vultures and their mass open graves, their decaying dead bodies and no one to attend to them. The king would assuage her anxiety with his sheer presence, love and concern, but all Neha could do was wait restlessly for the night to get over.

The days became troublesome because she was plagued with headaches and nausea. She started looking visibly sick. Meditation, chanting, breathing exercises and even anxiety-reducing medication were of little help. As soon as she got into the bed, the vultures would return, crying for help from a helpless Neha.

This phase would have passed without any serious impact on the kingdom or The Vultures but for an unfortunate and rather grave accident. One of the caddies, on returning from his village, had told the King of a bright light that people had seen over a waste dump. The inspection team sent by the King came back with a disastrous news. Soon after the sighting of the bright light, the entire area had caught fire.

Even after the fire had been diffused, people living in nearby villages started developing unusual symptoms. On reaching the spot, the King saw that hundreds of men, women and children had developed rashes on their skins; they complained of suffering from a burning sensation, nausea and discomfort. The king stayed there for almost a week to supervise relief work and organise medical facilities.

On investigating, it was found that a consignment from one of the pipelines had been contaminated with nuclear waste. It had happened again!

Whether it was a discarded weapon or the remnants of a nuclear power plant, the facts could not be ascertained. But the situation escalated and turned alarming when radioactivity in one of the dump yards increased rapidly and shot up beyond normal safety levels. All the people from the vicinity had to be hastily evacuated.

Almost immediately, the radioactivity levels started increasing in many of the other dumps. This was followed by more evacuations. All activities in the region had to be brought to a halt and all the pipelines had to be closed. Many people working in the yards developed symptoms of exposure to radioactivity. Factory after factory and recycling plant after recycling plant came to a grinding halt.

All the recycling stores worldwide had to be closed. Neha and her team feared that radioactivity could reach their products through the circular economy. The products in the stores were hastily taken out and buried deep in the ground to prevent possible leaks. All the recycled goods promoted by celebrities were found abandoned recklessly in dustbins across the world.

All this had a terrible impact on The Vultures. From soaring to the most dizzying heights of success, they came crashing down. The company was dying and all their operations were shut down. In a period of three months, only a dozen workers with suitable

protective gear were present in the field. They too were mostly engaged in detecting radioactivity with Geiger-Müller counters in their hand. The people in the countryside had fled to save their lives, as symptomatic cases increased. The capital city was transformed into a ghost town with the mass exodus of people. The closing down of factories and plants coupled with health hazards of the radioactivity had a crushing effect on the economy and the health parameters of the region. As more and more people fell sick, the health care system, which had never been that efficient even earlier, was unable to cope with the influx of patients.

King Ayola, Neha, the prince and the king's aunt continued to stay at the palace with rudimentary staff and caretakers. Kiran was the sole occupant of the guesthouse. A brigade of highly-paid managers lived at the site.

As radioactivity levels kept increasing, it became mandatory for everyone to live indoors and wear protective gear at all times. In the meanwhile, the king's aunt breathed her last, comfortably, in her sleep. She probably died a natural death, but conspiracy theories began to fly about furiously, claiming that she was the first royal to die of radiation.

A vast majority of elements have a stable core, with their neutrons, electrons and protons living in equilibrium. It is this sub-atomic equilibrium that makes the planet a stable structure, with stable molecules and compounds that form the building blocks of all inanimate and animate matter. This stability of the building blocks has probably created a conducive environment for life to evolve. No known celestial body has an environment conducive for the evolution of life and its facilitation into millions of life forms. Some elements, however, are unstable, heavy, radiating and ready for fission or fusion.

Uranium leads the pack, and this precious metal is enriched to produce power as well as destructive weaponry. Chernobyl and Fukushima are testimony to the destructive power of these unstable nuclear elements. Presently, the world has a stockpile of nuclear weapons that can destroy the planet, many times over. Nuclear power plants also have the capacity to cause major accidents. Moreover, the proliferation of nuclear matter progresses unabated, with authoritarian regimes and even terrorist organisations possessing plenty of nuclear arsenals. The handling of these deadly elements is not foolproof and many a times, there have been instances of irresponsible handling, inept storage and ruthless dumping.

Irresponsible handling created the grave situation that The Vultures were now trapped under. They had never envisaged this in their wildest dreams. They had been so careful, so stringent, with strict standard operating procedures in place. Errors are not completely avoidable, it was just that this error was a very costly one with terrible consequences.

International agencies and experts found it very difficult to identify the source of the contamination and ascertain the exact spread of its dissipation in the dump yards. The mixing of radioactive elements in smog, water sources, soil particles, sewage and dust had taken it far from the point of first deposition. Like a pandemic, it had swept across the nation, swiftly and exponentially, and the only way to protect everyone was mass exodus from the contaminated areas. Protective gear only went so far to minimise chances of exposure, and an early diagnosis and treatment was expensive. The half-lives of these radioactive materials ultimately lessen over a few decades. Until then, one has to live with the calamity.

For The Vultures, it was for now time to choose safety over their business. In any case, the business had already collapsed and their brand was now in tatters, associated with contamination and danger. The Vultures had several things to worry about: they had to plan on how to avoid facing prosecution, preventing penal action and avoiding bankruptcy. For Neha and King Ayola, the safety of their people was paramount. They also had to prepare for a large-scale decontamination exercise to save the future generations.

For now, the source of the contamination had to be detected, even if it had spread over millions of tonnes of waste and garbage lying all over the country. And that was going to be an uphill, if not an altogether impossible task.

Radioactivity is one of the least understood branches of science. On one hand, radioactive matter are risky to handle and on the other hand, their impact is long lasting, sometimes even for many generations. In addition to causing heat burns and damage to human organs, it has an effect on the double helix DNA, the basic chemical responsible for continuity of traits, which also helps humans and other life forms to adapt to the environment. The double helix is the basis raw material for evolution of all living beings, including humans. Damage to these fundamental blocks of life impacts generation after generation.

King Ayola had kept up a brave face. He had learnt to own up for his decisions and live with them. But Neha was worried. This was a crisis beyond her capacity to handle. Kiran, Brigette and even Sridhar were all feeling helpless. This time, Neha was no longer alone in this turmoil. Her husband, the king; the prince and their countrymen were the ones whose future was also being jeopardised. Often, she would feel low and depressed.

The source of the radiation had to be detected first, she judged. Its spread had to be determined, the area impacted had to be cordoned off and decontamination operations had to commence. It was a financial disaster for the company. But she envisaged that economic activity would never completely cease for her.

Meanwhile, the protests against The Vultures were swelling to mammoth proportions. The environmentalists, the leftists, the right-wingers, the young, as well as veterans, were joining the protests in large numbers. Not a day would go by without headlines highlighting this monumental failed experiment of synergising economics with ecology. It was projected as an opportunist company's draconian plan to make money out of the environment. The matter was discussed in the parliaments of many nations. The European Union and UN General Assembly had a special session on the magnitude of the crisis and its possible containment. The World Health Organisation issued a red alert in the region. Most of the MoUs signed by The Vultures were either recalled or put into abeyance. With popular opinion going against The Vultures, many authorities issued notices to the company and initiated damage suits.

The plea by The Vultures under the force majeure clause fell on deaf ears amidst the clamour of pressure groups, television debates and public sentiments. The Vultures were on the run, their offices worldwide were being shut with the same haste that they had been established when they were marching to glory. The Vultures disputed the scientists, academicians and legal experts, claiming that they would soon find a scientific solution and commence a huge decontamination operation. But no one was convinced. The only thing Neha had in her favour was her status as a royal, and sovereign privileges protected her from arrest.

Radioactivity leads to the formation of radon particles, which disperse in the air through the gradients created by temperature, wind direction and the earth's magnetism. As winter approached, radon particles were detected, moving from Africa to the cooler regions of Europe and North America. The developed world, which had till now considered the nuclear radiations in Central Africa a localised event, was suddenly very worried. Now, the threat of nuclear radiation was in their backyard; it was no longer a third-world problem. People were falling ill in every corner of the colder countries. The sickness caused by radioactivity was reported as far as North China, Japan, Scandinavia, and even Siberia.

It was not just humans who were affected. Crops, poultry, goat, sheep, pigs and cows too, faced the effects. Radon particles were moving unabated from place to place, city to city, country to country, putting more and more people, property, flora and fauna at risk. The concentration of radioactivity varied. An entire consignment of apples, an entire stretch of corn and a town on a hill slope would be impacted in varied areas, creating micro-zones of severe radioactivity. There were frantic attempts—in vain—to chase the radons away.

Healthcare resources in all the affected countries were under severe pressure; authorities were doing their best to ramp up facilities to treat the swelling numbers of patients, both young and old, who were queuing up in front of hospitals. As the radioactivity levels rose, advisories were issued to people to remain indoors. Some influential and wealthy citizens were reported to have built radioactivity-free bunkers to survive the radons.

The world was now at war with the radons.

It became normal for people to carry equipment with them to measure radioactivity while venturing outdoors. All food, all crops, every piece of meat had to be checked for radiation prior to consumption. Children were born with dismal abnormalities. In a few nations, young couples were advised not to procreate. There was chaos everywhere; the world was crumbling under the weight of this nuclear onslaught. Economies were collapsing as demand for health care was increasing with each passing day. During summers, the radons would settle down. But come winter or a windy day, and the radons would again disperse from one place to another. With a half-life running into years, the radons remained potent for a long time. And, it didn't look as if there was a permanent or quick-fix solution to this critical problem.

When one batch dispersed, more appeared. More radons were emerging, and would continue to emerge, from the waste dumps of Central Africa.

Neha and King Ayola were living bang in the midst of it all—at the source, so to speak. It was challenging, troubling and distressing with every passing day. Neha was still trying her best to stay calm in the face of all that was happening. Her real challenge was yet to surface.

The king was still outwardly jovial and loving. However, all was not well. He had started to show symptoms of exposure to radiation. He developed heat burns all over his skin. A constant stomach upset and loss of appetite made him lose weight drastically. He looked weak and frail and had suddenly aged, looking much older than his years.

Neha was shattered by the king's condition. Guilt had already built its walls within her with the first accident, but now it was

shaking her at the core of her being. But she put all her emotions aside.

For now, she needed to focus on her husband, on restoring his well-being. She accompanied him to Europe to seek treatment in the best hospitals there.

Since King Ayola's condition was so serious and it entailed them travelling and being away from home, the prince was placed in the custody of Jennifer and her partner in Milan. During a visit to Romania, Jennifer had adopted a daughter; a gypsy girl who had been orphaned due to the civil war raging through the country. Jennifer's daughter and the prince were of the same age, and they got along very well. The kids were happy in each other's company. This was a huge relief for Neha. After having lavished all her love and care on the little prince, she felt assured that she had placed him in the best hands. Now, she could concentrate on devoting herself to her husband, as his full-time nurse.

But each medical diagnosis and report brought discouraging news. King Ayola had suffered organ damage, only rehabilitation and not recovery was contemplated. Neha was now nursing him like a mother. She was with him round the clock, ministering to his every need and trying to keep his spirits up.

They watched hundreds of movies on a projector at their villa at a medical retreat site. When the king felt energetic on an odd day, he insisted on going to the gym and slowly walking on the treadmill or lifting a few light dumbbells. It was his attempt to slowly gravitate towards good health and happiness. They also drifted to a nearby golf course, where the king had to use a battery-operated golf cart to move from one hole to the other. He was happy there, using an iron from the tee to play a full game. He could no longer use the wood. Neha ensured that she was always a shot behind the king.

After they finished their game, they had to go to different changing rooms. There were no private changing lounges for them in this medical retreat, and no nostalgic returns to their love were possible at this retreat, frequented by old couples making the most of their twilight years.

The king was aware that his presence, because of his exposure, was endangering Neha too. One early morning, in the wee hours before dawn, Neha woke up suddenly after an awful dream. She was shocked to find Ayola not by her side. She hurriedly switched on the light, jumped out of bed and checked the bathroom. But he wasn't there either. She opened the cupboard and found his backpack missing, as well as his clothes.

She stood looking around the room, her heart racing. She saw that he'd left his phone behind; it was lying on a table charging. And then, she spotted a note. He had left a small handwritten note authorising Neha to be the Regent in his absence, until time came for the prince to shoulder his responsibilities. He had also personally requested Neha not to search for him. This was the last straw.

Neha collapsed under the weight of her guilt. She was caged by it. She had injected so much pain... so much despair to the man whom she loved so deeply and madly.

The guilt was crushing her. She lay on the bed, weeping, loud sobs tearing through her body. She could barely breathe. Everything was her fault. If she hadn't been so ambitious, if she hadn't wanted to grow The Vultures so fast, if she had only been more careful...

It was as if the weight of the world's problems now rested on her frail shoulders. She was responsible for this. She had

unleashed this radon monster onto the world. And now the person she loved more than anyone in the world had fallen a victim to her ambition.

14

Tandav—The Dance of Shiva

Now, but for the prince, Neha felt she had no reason to live. When her husband had been by her side, she had mustered the courage to face the world. She had held on to the strength to go out and fight. She had been a strong leader, and even with their world crumbling around them, her team had stayed faithful to her because they trusted her implicitly.

All this while, the team had been burning both ends of the candle to find a solution to the horrific problem they had created. Yet, they had believed that under Neha's stewardship, they would bounce back. But now it all looked like a distant dream, an almost impossible feat, because their leader had become a shadow of her former self.

After months of mental exhaustion and a sense of complete helplessness, Neha had lost her spark, her joie de vivre. There was no light in her eyes, no spring in her step. It was as if she was merely existing, not living. After the king's disappearance, she had moved in with Jennifer, since the prince was there. Her best friend was shocked by the change she saw in Neha. She and her partner tried their very best to make Neha happy. However, they failed miserably.

Each day, Neha sat quietly, silent, a sad expression on her face, as if weighed down by the burdens of the world. She hardly smiled and when she did speak, it was in monosyllables.

But there was one bright spot in the darkness that was Neha's life and that was the kids. Their innocence, their demands and their boundless energy would occasionally bring Neha out of her shell. Her depression would melt away for a while as she played, sang and danced with the children. She would walk them to school, sit in a garden nearby until the bell rang and then walk them back home.

Lately she had started taking a mat and her beads along with her. She would lay out the mat under the shadow of a tree, sit cross-legged, close her eyes and chant to calm herself. Days, weeks and months passed in this manner. Deep inside, Neha was devastated. Life held no meaning for her. Her only anchor were the children and her prayers. Chanting in the garden in the midst of nature soothed and calmed her bruised soul.

Kiran was still in Africa, doing his best to fight the emissions. His team ventured across all the dumps in protective gear in an attempt to track and confine the radioactive matter that had started it all. He was also tasked with taking on the legal challenges that had come their way. With Neha away, he busied himself in engaging with lawyers and fighting suits from all over the world. The task was difficult enough because they were facing far too many suits. Further their dwindling finances and the absence of support from Neha made it worse. Kiran often came to Milan to meet Neha. He would keep her updated on everything that was happening. However, a disinterested, disillusioned and lost Neha said nothing. She showed no interest whatsoever in what was left of The Vultures. She felt no connection with what was once her brainchild.

Jennifer was dismayed at her friend's descent into depression and her indifference. It hurt her to see Neha so lifeless and sad. On her birthday, she managed to persuade Neha to come along with them for a picnic. Neha reluctantly agreed, not wanting to disappoint her friend and the children, who were eagerly looking forward to the outing. They went to a lakeside resort and were joined by several friends of Jennifer and her partner. They drank, played music, lit a bonfire, danced and sang all night.

Neha tried to summon up an occasional smile. She didn't want to be a wet blanket and ruin her friend's birthday celebrations. She tried her best to engage with people, but found the effort too taxing. She sat at a table overlooking the dark glistening lake, surrounded by chatter and music, the clinking of glasses, the clatter of plates and cutlery. As the moon shone across the still waters, Neha sat in a pensive mood, her chin resting in her hand, oblivious to the happiness all around her. Neha thought of her mother, her father, Brigette, Ruzbeh, Sridhar, Kiran and King Ayola. How disappointed they must be with me, she told herself.

The next day, she was sitting under a tree in the garden, meditating. Suddenly Saraswati popped up in her mind. Each and every word he had spoken, each and every story he had narrated and each and every image she remembered of him, flashed through her mind like a film. She didn't move an inch. She stayed in the garden, watching the reels, pausing and moving

forward in her mind's scope. She did not bother to buy herself lunch from the nearby store, a habit she had gotten into in the past few months. Hours passed and she continued to sit there motionless, forgetting to even pick up the kids from school. They were escorted home by a neighbour. When a worried Jennifer came in search of her, she found Neha under the tree, her eyes closed, tears softly streaming down her cheeks. It was well past midnight.

The next day, it was as if some miraculous transformation had taken place. Neha woke up vibrant and cheerful, a smile plastered on her face. She was her lively, confident old self. Jennifer and her partner were surprised but hesitantly thrilled by the transformation. After breakfast, Neha took out her laptop and got busy.

After a while, she informed Jennifer that she had booked a ticket to New Delhi. From there she was off to Gangotri, the source of the holy river Ganges, and then off on a long trek in the Himalayas. Jennifer was quite taken aback and wondered aloud about Neha travelling on her own in such a state. But Neha dismissed her fears. She wanted to do this, needed to do this.

She was on her own now. And she yearned to go to the mighty Himalayas, to the sacred Gangotri, and have a dip in the icy waters of the river Ganges to purge herself of everything that had happened to her. Neha's personal visit to India was booked at such short notice that the paparazzi never got wind of her travel plans. She landed unnoticed in New Delhi and took a taxi to Gangotri. The roads had improved, and after a night halt at picturesque Rudraprayag, she reached Gangotri by the afternoon. It took her two days to trek to Gaumukh, the point where the ice melts into water, the origin of the stream that eventually becomes the Ganges, the purest and most divine of all rivers.

At Gaumukh, she managed to rent a blanket and a shawl from the sole tea stall and proceeded to Tapovan, where Chaudhary Baba had reportedly moved more than a decade back. She would find him there if he was still alive. The trek to Tapovan was extremely rough as there were no pathways. She had to traverse through a narrow icy stretch alone to reach the base of the frosty, rock-strewn glacier. After hours of climbing, and a night spent under the warmth of a lone blanket, she ultimately reached the cave where Chaudhary Baba lived.

Chaudhary Baba seemed to have been waiting for Neha to arrive. As she stepped into the mouth of the cave, she saw a bearded man getting a fire ready with dried twigs, to provide her warmth and comfort. Chaudhary Baba looked just like what she had envisioned from the fables she had heard from Saraswati when she was a child, and before him, from Manik. The saint had a long beard and uncombed, matted hair. The only item of clothing he wore was a loincloth, even in the freezing temperatures of Tapovan.

Chaudhary Baba provided a sense of continuity for various generations of her clan. He seemed to know her entire family tree. Neha felt rooted and connected to the cosmos in the presence of the mystic.

The saint was very solicitous. He prepared a herbal mix and gave it to her. Not only did it provide instant comfort to Neha, but it also had some sort of miraculous effect as she no longer felt cold and exhausted.

She sat, rejuvenated, and began to narrate her story to Chaudhary Baba, who sat in a lotus posture on the ground and

listened attentively. 'Why did this happen to me and how do I resolve this?' Neha enquired once she was finished with the tale.

Chaudhary Baba smiled serenely and said, 'Think of it often and then act on it.' His words inadvertently reminded of Ayola, which brought tears to her eyes.

She began to sob and plaintively asked, 'Why am I responsible for causing so much pain to the people I love the most? Why am I in this pitiable situation?'

'Think of Shiva and He will guide you,' said the saint in a calm voice.

Neha closed her eyes and fervently prayed to Shiva. The image of a youthful face with Nandi the bull, a conch, a trishul, a snake, wet matted hair, a damru (small drum), a tiger lazing in the grass and a cloud of smoke, appeared before her. A dancing Shiva, a Shiva at ease with his wife Parvati, Shiva with his sons Ganesh and Karthikeyan, Shiva killing the demons and a meditating Shiva at Mount Kailash. A montage played before her eyes as she sat on the bare floor, focusing intently on the task at hand.

'You are still missing out on something significant. Search for it in Shiva,' whispered the sage. And suddenly, Neha was concentrating on his form. Shiva's eyes, the rudraksha garland, his muscular body and his blue neck. It was bluer than his body. Shiva calmly held all the poison the world released in his throat.

'Why the poison?' Neha asked the saint.

Chaudhary Baba took a deep breath and narrated a story.

A long time ago, the poison (*vish*) and the life-giving nectar (*amrit*) were mixed into the ocean. They had to be separated to save the life forms. The poison had to be removed, then isolated and protected, so that it would not spoil the waters. Each particle of poison had to be tracked, purified and removed from the ocean.

The gods had to find a solution. It seemed like an impossible task, but it had to be done. Since each and every material has a unique frequency at which it precipitates, the gods or the devatas decided that they would churn the ocean at a great speed, making the poison precipitate. Then they would again churn it, making it precipitate the lost nectar. The devatas alone would get the nectar, and the poison would be secured and they would protect it. And so, this was a must.

The devatas acquired the nectar and the mighty Shiva became the storehouse of the poison. He could, if he chose, use it on an appropriate target—at the right time and for a right cause.

Neha stayed on at Tapovan, surviving by drinking Chaudhary Baba's herbal concoction. One morning, she stepped out and was gazing at the snow-kissed mountains. She couldn't find the Baba. Neha looked around and suddenly, to her dismay, spotted a trail of people slowly moving uphill. They carried cameras, filming equipment and rations. They were dressed in mountaineering gear. A few of them wore uniforms and were carrying guns. Chaudhary Baba was nowhere to be seen. The world had found Neha.

She stared at the crowd snaking their way up the icy mountains. She was in a state of shock. How had this happened? How had they found her in this remote region? Was there nowhere she could escape to, away from the ugly hordes of paparazzi for whom she was nothing but clickbait—someone who could sell their magazines and newspapers, increase their TRPs and drive traffic to their channels and websites? They didn't care about her or even look at her as someone dealing with remorse and sorrow.

The paparazzi took hundreds and thousands of pictures of her, filming her from all possible directions, zooming in on her

tired eyes and her frostbitten fingers, as she sat there defeated but defiant. The men in uniform were part of the Border Security Force. After a while, she collapsed. The jawans laid her cold, exhausted body onto a stretcher equipped with oxygen cylinders to comfortably bring her back to the foothills. From there, a helicopter was arranged to transport her to Dehradun airport, from where she was flown to Delhi in an air ambulance. Neha spent almost a week in the army hospital to regain her energy.

But the world was not going to let her live in peace. The media was pressuring her to talk about the disaster. Once she had recovered, she agreed to hold a press conference. Hordes of international press teams arrived in New Delhi to attend the press conference, which was organised at the sprawling Ramlila grounds. Neha stood alone on the stage, looking pale and exhausted. But she straightened her spine, jutted her chin out, and stood, seemingly composed and calm. She politely answered every question and bravely declared that she and she alone could solve the problem of nuclear contamination. She acknowledged her own errors and her culpability in what had occurred. But now, she declared that the world leaders would have to cooperate with her to find a solution, failing which humanity was doomed to perish under the weight of the problem.

A hush of shocked silence fell across the jam-packed maidan. Was this to be the end of the world as they knew it? Neha watched silently as the assembled media slowly emerged from their shock and began to buzz with more questions, each of them thrown at her like sharpened arrows. She smiled weakly and stated, 'I have said what I had to. Now it's up to the world's leaders to cooperate.'

She turned and hastily left the stage, leaving behind a stunned audience.

With nuclear waste and radiation threatening the very existence of the planet, The Vultures worked hard on finding a solution to the seemingly impossible task of reining in the waste, dealing with it and restoring the world to a safer, greener entity. After months of research and a lot of hard work and dedication, they finally came up with a solution. The Vultures would make the largest centrifuge ever envisaged, to churn the waste and isolate each of its components, including the radioactive poison. The useful materials and poison would be separated and the nuclear material secured. Once the nuclear material was tracked, separated, secured and stored in a protected place, things would quickly return to normal. The centrifuge could be used time and again to solve such eventualities in the future too.

With Neha's idea, negotiating skills and her still-steady repute, they managed to get the Indian government to pledge technical and financial support to The Vultures.

The possible success of The venture was examined, and soon many more nations extended their support as well. After all, it was in everyone's interests to see this hazardous problem, which threatened the earth's very existence, solved. Kiran was already preparing the blueprint of the equipment. Parts of the mega centrifuge were being fabricated at different global locations. The world had not seen such collaboration in the recent past. Humanity had come together before and stood united to repair the ozone holes and then to keep a watch on extra-terrestrial events by establishing a grand telescope. And yet, this was a unique situation. With worldwide collaboration and assistance, the individual parts were transported to Central Africa, so that this giant equipment could be assembled in less than three months time.

Finally, the centrifuge was erected and operations commenced. A hush washed over the planet. It began: whirring and churning, different materials were sprung at different frequencies. When the rotation speed was increased, complex matter got broken down into their building blocks. The metals, the organic matter, the petro-chemicals, bio-waste and e-waste were breaking, and their components precipitating at different speeds. The explosives, inflammables, heavy metals and the unstable and radioactive materials were separated.

After its initial success, the equipment was moved from dump yard to dump yard till the entire mountain of waste was churned and separated.

The waste was no longer the same. Now, it was segregated and isolated into its components. The churning had converted waste into wealth. And in the process, the poisons, dangerous elements and the nuclear matter were also secured. The churning went on for months together, until the time came when each and every particle of the radioactive substance was precipitated and stored in a sealed, impenetrable box.

The nuclear matter was much more than what they had imagined. As investigations commenced to find out the reason for the sabotage many conspiracy theories were floated. What had actually happened was that too many—not just one—terrorist organisations and irresponsible nuclear powers had used the opportunity to get rid of unsafe materials from their backyard, not realising the consequences of their actions. Thus, it was destined that the nuclear matter would leak during its long-piped journey. It was unfortunate that the irresponsibility of terrorists and rogue nations had created such a catastrophe.

Neha and King Ayola's kingdom had already become a repository of the valuable metals, minerals and alloys extracted from the waste. The composting of organic matter had created a rich harvest that transformed the land in the country. It had, overnight almost, made available thousands of hectares of fertile earth for agriculture, horticulture and animal husbandry. The jungles were regenerating and the forests were once again brimming with wildlife. The factories and foundries were working with renewed vigour. The centrifugation had changed the fundamental game plan. There was no need for recycling anymore, because now, the waste was being reconverted to its building blocks, which could be used to create things that were new. The country which had faced devastation and been turned into a wasteland, was now rejuvenating... sprouting the roots and shoots of sustainable growth.

Now that the problem had been solved, Neha was once again in the limelight, this time as a popular and much-loved celebrity, and was hailed as a saviour. She had been restored to her former glory by a fickle media and an equally fickle populace. She was given an offer to contest for the post of Secretary General of the United Nations, considering the goodwill she enjoyed. She was once again nominated for various awards. However, Neha had no interest in the affairs of the world. Too much had happened and she was still devastated by the disappearance of her husband. Her ideas had almost brought the world to the brink of destruction. It was something she could not forget or absolve herself of. She was now absorbed in a new and thankless mission.

Neha had become a propagandist of waste reduction rather than waste recycling. 'The world was consuming too much,' she said to the media. 'That was the real problem. Such high levels of consumption would naturally generate high levels of waste. The world had turned increasingly materialistic, cut off from nature, and human beings were losing their very essence.' Neha believed that the madness had to stop somewhere; with her, perhaps.

15

Pandora's Box

Now that the problem of waste was solved and The Vultures had re-settled, Neha decided to move on. The shares of the company were soaring. Her kingdom in Central Africa had become not only the depository of global waste, but had also become the source of all major minerals and compounds to build things needed by the economies of the world.

However, there was a catch.

The enormity of waste made centrifuging, reprocessing and reusing a nightmare, and it had its limits. At some level, the growth of waste generation had to be controlled. The endless cycle of greed had to stop. There had to be a limit set for waste production too. It was mandatory if mankind was to save the planet and ensure continuity of life on Mother Earth.

Mankind could not continuously generate waste. There was a limit to centrifuging, recycling and reassembling. The solution lay in waste reduction; this alone was a viable and sustainable solution to the Frankensteinian monster created through prolific consumption.

There was another issue. Neha now possessed a box full of secured radioactive material. It was critical and life-threatening. The box, if misused, had the power to shove humanity into a catastrophic situation. The captured radon particles were potent enough to threaten life on the planet wholesale. The box had dumped responsibility on Neha, as well as the power to bargain. No non-state player had such a privilege. The world leaders called it 'Pandora's Box'. The media roared: a regent of a Central African country personally had control of the nuclear arsenal. This was not permissible. It was too large a threat. Pandora's Box had to be stolen and diffused at the earliest.

Meanwhile, Neha was on a new path. She was setting goals for herself. Reducing her possessions, reducing waste and creating maximum out of minimal possessions.

Eventually, Neha had only twenty-one personal items in her possession, all of which could be packed into a backpack, and which weighed less than seven kilograms. This backpack was her world. It also included a smart watch which directly connected to Pandora's Box—Shiva's own blue neck. To use the poison against the targets, at the right time, and for the right purpose.

And Neha was ready to use the power of the box to bargain for a sustainable life on the planet. Failing which, the Shiva in her would dance, casting a spree of destruction to ensure submission.

Neha was now a nomad. She had no permanent address. She had given up control of The Vultures to Kiran. Her kingdom was now governed by the council of ministers. She was now a wandering monk, moving from city to city, place to place with her minimal belongings, preaching the message of a new world where personal possessions had the least value.

She would talk to children, liberating them from the burdens of greed and possession, encouraging them to learn the values of sharing and cooperation.

She would say, 'Materialistic possessions have a limit. They don't add value to life. They only add to clutter. This clutter makes you confused, mechanically dependent, perplexed and sick. One ultimately succumbs under its weight. The purpose of life is to move ahead and progressively abandon materialism behind.'

One day, Kiran called Neha. She was invited to talk at the United Nations General Assembly regarding her crusade.

Over the years, the United Nations General Assembly had seen its power and influence fading; it seemed more like a puppet entity. It had become a talk shop, where nations indulged in mudslinging their opponents and attempted to craft public opinion out of thin air. Occasionally, the UN proceedings would grab headlines, but when it came to wars, oppression, ethnic cleansing, terrorism, mafia, corruption, money laundering and human rights, they had limited influence. The superpowers of the world were still the key decision-makers.

Now that The Vultures had efficiently cleared up the problem of nuclear waste with their centrifuge solution, they were once again being feted and celebrated across the world. Neha's name and photos were splashed across newspaper front pages and magazine covers. She had been interviewed extensively by TV channels, and was always greeted with gushing admiration. Thanks to her success at saving the world from potential destruction or even mass extinction, the United Nations had invited her to deliver a keynote address on her contributions in solving environmental problems created by waste, and her success in solid waste management.

When the invite had been issued, they had expected mundanity. They could have never expected that this speech would make history and reduce the assembly to speechlessness and initiate one of the largest collaborations for waste reduction. Thanks to Neha's stature, her keynote address attracted a large audience; in fact, it was a full house at the assembly. She was probably the most accomplished speaker the United Nations General Assembly had ever invited to speak, other than a few powerful heads of governments. The media was also present in large numbers, jostling for space.

Whether vilified or put on a pedestal by the media, Neha had always attracted media attention owing to her path-breaking actions, her persona, her background and her ability to articulate her vision.

Normally, speakers in this august assembly would read from a paper and remain confined to the topic. Neha, however, veered from the norm. Her speech was impromptu, straight from the heart; and she spoke on a variety of subjects ranging from capitalism, business, faith, fame, the power of money, minimalism and many other aspects of life to a hushed and electrified audience.

'Money provides one with choice. A choice to be flamboyant and aggressive. It gives one an opportunity to be insane, arrogant and abusive. But the same money also gives one an opportunity to be humble, grateful, innovative and to lend a helping hand. We all need to make the latter choice. Moreover, with or without money, life still gives each one of us a choice to commit to a cause. The world assembly needs to discover the right cause and solicit the right direction for its member states.

'Humans have their origin in the hunter-gatherers. And it was the commune which provided them with protection as well as the capacity to hunt. They worked in groups and shared their game. Individuals supplemented and complemented each other. Later, an agricultural and pastoral society created value for land and vouchsafed an emphasis on family. Industrialisation ushered in the value of time and a collaborative mindset. It brought in the concepts of assembly lines and economies of scale, thus altering the matrix of human life forever. The information boom made individuals paramount.

'Today, personal possessions have become a hallmark of success. Possessing much more than what we require has become a human obsession. We are in a rat race to possess more. In the process, less than one percent of humanity presently possesses a majority of the world's wealth and capital. With regards to political power, it is further skewed. Similarly, fame has been monopolised, with very few cornering most of the lot. The vast majority are mango people, padded and waiting in line to play on an uneven pitch; the ones in the playfield have raised fences, preventing the entry of newcomers because they want it all. They want the lion's share of resources—be it money, health, name or fame—and they will do everything in their power to ensure that it remains with them. Thus, a cosy club of the ultra-rich, ultra-powerful and ultra-famous have captured the world's resources and now thrive off them, while the rest are left to suffer the consequences of their greed, eking out a living on too little. While the rich fly around in fancy jets and drive around in expensive gas-guzzling cars, never mindful of their carbon footprints, it is the poor who suffer the consequences: climate change, rising coastlines, increasing waste, meagre resources... The rich become richer and the poor become poorer. This is the way of the world and it will continue this way because of vested interests. It is an unequal, brutal power game and the ones who suffer the most are the poor.

'Humanity needs to climb out of this pit, and this era of greed for possessions needs to become a thing of the past. This race for materialism and possessing more and more, is only destroying our planet and widening the rift between the haves and have-nots. We need to progress to a rental economy. An economy that facilitates sharing.

'We all know that possessions inculcate inefficiencies. Sharing, on the other hand, is collaborative, efficient, equitable and need-based. Inefficiencies always make one lose the game of survival. If we do not correct ourselves, we will certainly lose as a species. Let human greed not overpower human intellect and human evolution. It is our divine duty to ensure the end of inefficiencies and promote the growth of participative ownership. This will not only make our societies more equitable, but will also help to heal planet earth.

'Our ignorance has converted us into waste-producing machines. We are robots fuelled by avarice and indifference, who only want to possess more... and more... and more... And at what cost? And why? Our homes, our warehouses, our godowns, our offices, all harbour enormous waste. We have created an inventory pile, and we waste an entire lifetime in our attempts to store and protect, this underused and unused pile of material possessions.

'Eventually, our possessions will be outdated, or they will expire and will be thrown back to nature. We need to know what we really require, and we have to possess. We miss out on time, experiences and enrichment due to our indulgence with inanimate, heartless and soulless objects. Humans need to own less and waste less—and we must do this to survive. Our recklessness is not only endangering our survival, but also the survival of mother earth. Our voracious greed is not only destroying us, our nature and the environment, but also all other living species. Moreover, by creating imbalances in the ecosystem, we are only contributing to our own destruction. It is the bounden duty of each nation state, each of you representatives, to take this agenda forward. The agenda of sharing and caring, of saying a resounding 'No' to insatiable consumption, caring for our planet and all beings. We do not have much time. We have already lost most of it.

'Nation states are an arrangement forged by us. They exist for administrative convenience. In reality, we are all connected. Each one impacts the other , one impacts everyone else. Hunger, indulgence, disease, extinction of species, destruction of habitats and the arrogance of a fistful of us is leaving craters of devastation on every individual. Those who do not believe in compromising their lifestyle and those who believe they are superior need to be shown a mirror of reality and be cut down to size. The ones who suffer in abject poverty, face subjugation and hellish conditions for survival, need to be lifted. The ones who believe that science and technology can solve all our problems need to be reminded of their ignorance. We all need to face reality. We all need to note what is really happening.

'We all have to channel our greed. The greed for materialistic possessions of this incremental order is hurtling us towards a catastrophe. The world will not have neighbourhood backyards to dump the products of our extravagance. We need to take the right path, and we need to do it now. The ones who do not follow this path or refuse it need to be annihilated. The ones who follow it need to be appreciated. Let the bad coin not chase the good coin anymore.

'We should now be working towards the reduction of waste by twenty percent every year. For this, we have to reduce all unnecessary possessions, rein back our greed and reduce the clutter around us. We have to remove the poisonous packaging and frills. These are extraneous and unnecessary, and only contribute to more waste and further degradation of the environment. We need to go local and try to consume what can be grown and produced locally. This would help reduce the carbon footprint of availing food, thereby promoting sustainability and ethical eating. We need to increase the use of renewable energy. The environment has been destroyed by us and we urgently need to restore it. Our cities have become concrete jungles where chaotic traffic, noxious fumes and unregulated waste have made them living hell. We need to plant trees to green our environment, use bicycles to lessen pollution, and remodel cities so that they are pedestrian-friendly. This would help in reducing greenhouse gases too.

'Each of us needs to do our bit to contribute to cleaning and greening our environment. We can start with composting and recycling the waste in our homes and in our own backyards. We should not be exporting our waste. We, The Vultures, have been talking about waste management all these years, but that is just so old-fashioned. The only way to move forward, to protect ourselves, our environment, other species and the earth is through waste reduction and that alone. Yes, waste reduction is the goal for all of us and that requires a huge commitment.'

Neha had started her speech softly, calmly listing each of her points. As the speech progressed, she grew more impassioned. Now she paused and looked around at the audience. They were sitting there—dumbstruck, awed and introspective. She softly began again, 'But, you know what?' They inched closer.

'Fear sometimes helps too. The fear of destruction, the fear of an angry Shiva, the Hindu God of Destruction—the fear of his destructive Tandav, his dance, and the fear of death. I have the global depository of radons in what I call my Pandora's Box. I will use it discreetly and selectively if anyone refuses to comply or cooperate.'

There was pin-drop silence, followed by gasps from the audience. Heads turned as they started murmuring and whispering to one another and soon, some started talking loudly. On the podium, Neha remained calm, standing straight and tall, almost like a statue. She looked around, and raised her hand, signalling for them to stop talking. A fearful hush fell over the hall. Neha continued in an icy voice, 'Please do not take this as an idle threat. My watch has the key to the Pandora's Box. I can use it if this collective vision is sabotaged.'

Saying this, Neha abruptly turned and walked off the stage with her head held high.

Nobody clapped and nobody rose to offer a vote of thanks for her marvellous speech. The assembly was left aghast and shocked. Neha left the room and walked back to the portico of the building to get into her car. No one came to see her off.

After a few days, Neha returned to Central Africa with renewed purpose. She became utterly engrossed in a massive plan to convert the vast lands, which had been destroyed and turned into a desert land, into agricultural fields with the help

of compost made ready from organic waste.

Initially, the world powers tried to come up with plans to dispossess Neha of the Pandora's Box—bribe her or steal it away. It had to be taken away from someone as dangerous as her. There were also secret plans to track Neha and annihilate her, making it so that the threat would die with her. However, public opinion was with Neha. People believed that she was using her position for a good cause, that she was persuading every individual to take suitable action to save the world from environmental disaster. Neha had garnered a huge amount of goodwill to support this proposal.

She was by far, more trusted than all the other political leaders of the world put together. People around the world were rallying around her to support her agenda, and protesting against naysayers. The good coins were now chasing the bad. The people knew that they were on the brink of a disaster and realised that Neha was right. It was now up to them to do something. The power was in their hands.

Neha, in the meanwhile, withdrew from the spotlight and concentrated on her duties as a regent. King Ayola had always wanted to initiate the process of democratisation of the kingdom, with communities being at the epicentre of a participative democracy, building the quintessence grassroots leadership. He had been waiting for an opportue time.

The Central African kingdom was emerging as a leading producer of agricultural and forest produce. It was also establishing well-planned cities and building a prosperous countryside. It was time to bring his vision to fruition.

Neha worked day and night to make the kingdom economically prosperous and politically vibrant, without undermining the strengths of its communities. She wanted to preserve its social fabric, its rich culture, age-old tradition and the freedom of its individuals. In contrast to a human-centric paradigm of growth, Neha attempted to build a holistic model of development of communities along with preserving the environment and all its flora, fauna and inanimate elements.

The United Nations, in the meanwhile, had set a target to reduce waste by a quarter in three hundred and sixty-five days. Individual targets were set for individual states, which further allotted reduction targets to each province, each city and every household. It was easy to calculate the total quantum of the waste as now most of it was finding its way to the kingdom and to Neha. The vast network of pipelines made it possible to gauge the source and type of waste at the point of entry.

Soon, a new system of packaging was evolved, which was biodegradable and sustainable. Communities were encouraged to grow locally what they consumed. The farm-to-fork concept was becoming increasingly popular and people became more aware of the carbon footprint and provenance of the food they consumed. Communities started putting aside even small patches of lands to productive use. Terrace gardens too became increasingly popular and a large swathe of people were producing their own food. Individual houses started setting up their own waste composting units and waste management consultants were being hired to reduce, reuse and recycle waste generated in homes and workplaces.

Waste was no longer taken for granted. It was no longer considered someone else's problem. A vast majority of humanity knew that they were accountable for the waste they produced, they were accountable for the degradation of the planet and they

had the power to bring about change. A change that would save the planet, its flora and fauna, including human life.

Micro-incineration and micro-gasification plants were being installed worldwide. Community participation vis-à-vis waste had become a people's movement.

In the first year of the UN resolution itself, the waste reaching dumps, landfills and other such sinks stood reduced to such an extent that it was below the set target. The world leaders stopped viewing Neha as evil; they realised that her intentions were good. So, they started working on achieving the targets. It was also politically correct to toe this line as the world over, people shared Neha's concerns. The threat of the Pandora's Box looming over them had changed the world; humanity was able to resolve one of the major catastrophes faced by it through its resolve, even though its efforts had been provoked by the shadow of a danger that had threatened to subsume it. Just like repairing ozone holes and the decline in build-up of devastating dangerous nuclear arsenal, people were now winning the battle against waste.

Waste reduction also brought in a more equitable world. The desire for endless material possessions was slowly but firmly being diluted. People now wanted to experience life, live in the moment and experience the contentment of living in a collective, collaborative community. Once where private possessions were paramount, now sharing was seen as a much sought-after way of life. The mad rush to keep up with the Jones or even outshine them was long gone.

Life took on a more measured rhythm: savoured for the beauty of nature, the quiet contentment of shared moments with family and friends, more time was contemplated for doing things that people loved instead of a stressful, chaotic existence defined by crass materialism. Unnecessary possessions, irrational attachment to inanimate objects, piling, hoarding and clutter became old-fashioned, paving the way for a new world order.

16

Return to Paradise

The hectic life of the Regent was however, devoid of love, affection and warmth. To begin with, Neha considered being alone as a blessing in disguise; after all, she had enemies in high places. Even though Neha had decided that the Pandora's Box would not be needed, she was still dreaded. Now, it stood as a symbol of the people's weapon against arrogance and the irrational and irresponsible actions of the rich and powerful.

However, she did not want to jeopardise the safety of her son, the prince, who lived away in a loving home with Jennifer. King Ayola, she intuitively knew, was shouldering a burden similar to hers. He would not return until he had fully recovered and would not want to be a threat to his family.

Jennifer and her family spent a few weeks with Neha. After a long time, the palace was once again filled with joy and life. Neha was reunited with her precious son. He had grown a few inches taller and looked more and more like his father with every passing day. She spent the next few days exclusively with the prince. They spent time in the library, where she read him books that he didn't understand. She took him golfing, but the prince was more interested in chasing the ball than hitting it. He loved being with his mother nonetheless, and did not want to let go of her hand. Neha was finally content and at peace.

She desperately wanted her husband to return. Finding him and bringing him home would be her only priority, she decided.

One morning, after Neha and the prince have had breakfast, he returned to his bedroom for his mid-morning nap. As per her routine, Neha was reading the newspaper, glancing through an article on a possible civil war brewing in one of the neighbouring countries. She was trying to analyse and weigh the impact of this on her nation, when a staff member politely interrupted her.

He handed her an anonymous parcel. It had her name and address written in neat, legible block letters; with no return details. She opened it and found an album of photographs.

Neha stared at it and wondered—had Sridhar sent it? But he would have told her, and he would have certainly written his address. It was not Jennifer or Brigette's handwriting. Kiran was too occupied to surprise her like this. Was this a message from the king? She so desperately wanted the king to reappear the same way as he had left. Who could it possibly be if not him? After a deep breath, she opened the album to solve the mystery.

The album was filled with original photographs that had been printed and laminated. There was a picture of her addressing the United Nations General Assembly. She looked defiant and calm. The next photo was of her wedding ceremony in Vaitheeswaran Koil. Sridhar was handing over the thali to King Ayola to tie it around Neha's neck.

Tears welled up in her eyes when she thought back of that day and how much she had missed her father's presence. After

her mother's death, Saraswati had effortlessly taken care of her. All he had wanted was for Neha to be happy and wedded. He would have been elated to see this day if he was alive. Perhaps things would have been a lot different too.

The next photo was a candid shot of Neha sitting in a boat by the Ganges, staring at a matka (mud pot) adorned with flowers and capped with a red cloth. The matka held her father's ashes. She looked lonely and distraught. After his death, she had to pick up her life and start afresh, and she recalled it with a sad determination.

The next set of images gave her goose bumps. They were images of her in Mumbai. She was sitting alone, and in the stark background was a small baby vulture. It was taken at Ruzbeh's funeral. It was the genesis of everything that followed.

There was a photograph of her sitting by the window of a train, her hair flying as she enjoyed the cool breeze in the king's private salon. She was visibly in love. This voyage had triggered a new journey. Both the pictures of her on the cover of *Forbes* were present. Then there was one of hers and the king at the Nobel Prize award ceremony. This, unlike the other pictures that had been leaked by the paparazzi, was special. The king was caressing Neha's gentle baby bump. He was gazing at her with affection. She had felt very secure and loved in that moment.

This picture had not gone public.

If it had, it would have confirmed her secret to all the rumour mongers. Someone had intentionally kept this a secret.

She felt a sense of gratitude towards this anonymous admirer.

There were hundreds of pictures, each better than the other, bringing back the most important phases of her life. The photographer must have taken thousands of frames. He must have spent a lifetime capturing these candid moments and choosing the best of them. There were photographs of her with all those who mattered—Ayola, the prince, Jennifer, Brigette, Sridhar, Ruzbeh, Kiran, and even Ramlal. There were photographs of her ancestral house in Hisar. There was even a photograph of her climbing to Tapovan, surrounded by icy glaciers and snow-capped peaks. Surprisingly, there was no image of Chaudhary Baba. He probably never existed in a physical, three-dimensional form. He could only be experienced and felt.

Eventually there was this photograph that held great significance to Neha. It depicted King Ayola gracefully emerging from the entrance of a rehabilitation centre in Ukraine. The address of the centre was clearly in focus. The king was in Chernobyl where he was being treated. He looked healthy. A thrilled Neha was already halfway to Chernobyl in her thoughts, thudding with excitement to join the king and bring him back. She could already feel his arms around her.

There was one image left, and after this gift, Neha wondered who this person was. It wasn't Ayola. Someone had been tracking her with a close lens and had captured moments that truly defined her. Moments that had shaped her life the way it was. She felt a sense of déjà vu and attachment, a sense of connection and belonging. She did not want the album to end, yet was equally curious to see the last image.

The last image was different. It was the only image that had a note attached to it. She flipped the page and her whole body shook. A heavy weight fell on her shoulders; she forgot to breathe for a moment.

It was the original photograph published in *The New York Times*. The intimate image of her and Jennifer intertwined in a

passionate embrace. The very image that had given a full-blown spin to the roller-coaster of her life. Beneath it was a handwritten note.

In block letters were three words: I AM SORRY.

Acknowledgements

My thanks are due to Vinitha Nayar, Sandhya Sridhar, Sandhya Ravishankar, Ranjit Roy Choudhury, Anurag & Venu Sehgal, Shailendra Garg and M.T.S Dinakaran. My heartfelt gratitude to my publisher and my editors in assisting me while bringing out this book. I would also like to thank my father, Dr. Sarva Daman, wife Pallavi and my daughters, Indrani and Ishita, for their constant support.

Reviews of Oxygen Manifesto

Chennai Express

28-03-2019 THURSDAY

ECO-CENTRIC TALES FROM THE OFFICE OF A BUREAUCRAT

● Roshne Balasubramanian

The earth, as we know it, is crumbling right beneath our feet, and we need a trigger, to inspire a new generation of 'earth warriors'. So, what can one do about it? "At the basic level, reinforce learning—about environmental development and sustainability," says Atulya Misra, a senior officer of the Indian Administrative Services. The bureaucrat, in his role as the Additional Chief Secretary, Revenue and Disaster Management Department, Government of Tamil Nadu, has authored his debut book *Oxygen Manifesto - A Battle for the Environment* for the very purpose of strengthening our connection with the environment.

"After 20 years of bureaucracy, I was back into the academic circle. I was doing a course in Public Policy where sustainable development was key. We were introduced to people like Amartya Sen and Shashi Tharoor. What I found was, a lot of people were writing in addition to their full-time profession. So, six years ago, I decided to write a book on waste management. But, a few chapters were all that I could pen down," he shares.

When Atulya attended a talk by author Jeffrey Archer, his perspectives found clarity. "Archer asked the audience if they have ever thought of writing a book, and how many have actually taken the step to write one. I pondered over it," he recalls.

Pallavi, his wife, joins the conversation, "We have been married for 25-odd years, and from day one, he has always said that he wants to write a book."

"Yes, it has been a long-time desire. But the urge increased when I became closely involved with environment-related activities. I started creating characters for my book. There are several good non-fiction books written about the environment. I wanted to write a book that was emotional and humane," concurs Atulya, who has also held other highly designated posts.

His writing is engaging, and its potato chip chapters are easily digestible. Much like the earth, the book has several layers, and the story about environmental degradation and the impact of the Anthropocene takes us on a journey from its very core to the crust of the issues.

'...The ecological and cultural diversity is reducing at an exponential rate over the last few decades. Man is promoting tailored species of plants and animals for its needs and requirements at the cost of natural diversity. The genetically modified plants, animals and microbes have the capacity to become Frankenstein monsters...,' he writes.

The narrative is knitted with issues plaguing the environment, ideas which are considered fringe in today's times but are bound to emerge as mainstream thought in the future, an undercurrent of minimalism and veganism, leadership, displaced people, alternate philosophy and alternate lives; an element of travel, and water footprint. But in the backdrop of all the eco-centric dialogues are two characters leading the battle for the environment.

"The characters are concerned, and in their journey, they sacrifice many things. The aim of the book is to create a dialogue on environment reconstruction as a paramount duty of every human being," he shares. The author in his book has deliberately kept away from routine politics and focused solely on the environment.

"In the book, you will find shades of me and other officers and people who have inspired me. I have tried my best to keep the work as realistic as possible," he says.

Atulya worked on the book for four months. "This was quite a learning experience. I am also planning to write a book on disaster management," he says.

(The book is available on www.amazon.in)

About the book

Oxygen Manifesto - A Battle for the Environment is a story of the triumph of ordinary people over the might of the establishment in their battle to save the environment. Atulya worked on the book for four months. "I am also planning to write a book on disaster management," he says.

THE HINDU METROPLUS

CHENNAI • Wednesday • May 29, 2019

Keeping it real
Author Atulya Misra places the marginal under a spotlight
• SPECIAL ARRANGEMENT

Stories from the margins

IAS officer Atulya Misra's book *Oxygen Manifesto* tries to make a case for environmental issues in India

:: MEGHNA MAJUMDAR

You would expect a book titled *Oxygen Manifesto: A Battle for the Environment* (Rupa Publications) to hit the ground running with climate change statistics and species endangerment episodes. But, for a long portion of his early pages, IAS officer-turned author Atulya Misra talks about people. About island tribes in the Andamans and temple festivals in Tamil Nadu, fishing communities in Manipur and vegan lifestyles on the move, and a man in Manipur they call Thatha.

This was a deliberate decision by the author, not to draw the reader in to make the cause relatable, but to put the marginal under a spotlight. "Environmental issues themselves are marginal issues, in the current political scenario," he points out, "My idea was to take everything from the margins to the centre." Moreover, he adds, "The environment cannot be seen in isolation. It has to have a social context, a political context...the philosophy of life and the general culture of the nation is associated with it." So the book describes these real, lesser-known lives and philosophies, but through the eyes of fictional protagonists. The story itself is fictional, but is peppered with hundreds of intriguing little facts about various Indian communities and their relationship with land and Nature.

Take, for instance, the character called Thatha, based on the family history of a friend of Misra's daughter. "When I asked him how he knew not only Hindi, but a number of other North Indian languages quite well, he told me that his father, though Tamilian, was from Manipur. He told me of a district there, called More, which had a significant Tamil population. I later found out that about 6 lakh people from various parts of Tamil Nadu are settled in that district. That is how the character of Thatha was created. There is a bit of Sunderlal Bahuguna in him. There are people like him around us, actively trying to plant trees and preserve Nature against disaster, out of sheer affection and possessiveness for their surroundings. But their stories are confined to the regions they belong to." This character is Atulya's way of giving such regional heroes their due.

Oxygen Manifesto: A Battle for the Environment is available at all major bookstores and online on Amazon and Flipkart.

> The environment cannot be seen in isolation. It has to have a social context, a political context...the philosophy of life is associated with it

EXCLUSIVE INTERVIEW: MLA KULDEEP SENGAR'S WIFE
UNNAO RAPE SURVIVOR'S UNCLE MANIPULATED HER

JOURNALISM WITH A HUMAN TOUCH | www.theweek.in | TheWeekMag | TheWeekLive | ₹50

THE WEEK

FREE 36-PAGE SUPPLEMENT
BUDGET 2019: INVEST BETTER, SAVE MORE

KERALA
A YEAR AFTER THE DELUGE

Manifesto for Mother Earth

BY NIRMAL JOVIAL

Is it the responsibility of the governments alone to protect nature? And, what roles can ordinary people play to conserve the environment? *Oxygen Manifesto*, a masterfully-crafted book by Atulya Misra IAS, not only explores these questions but also presents a policy statement for a new-age green movement.

Blending both fictional and non-fictional narrative styles, *Oxygen Manifesto* tells the story of Thatha, a Tamil man settled in Manipur, and Ravi Chandran Bose, an IAS officer from Tamil Nadu posted in Manipur.

Misra ingeniously sets the scene using history and culture. For example, the second chapter tells the reader how "non-Mongoloid dark-skinned Tamil-speaking inhabitants" came to Moreh in Manipur. There is fine detailing about each character, too. With his passion and willpower, Thatha single-handedly changes the landscape of Moreh by planting trees. Thatha's simple life and Ravi's love for nature are fed to the reader subtly.

As the story proceeds, Ravi creates a movement, with Thatha's blessings, that will soon become the greatest environmental project in the country. The idea presented by Ravi is a mix of direct civil action and decentralisation.

The 'circles'—communes of climate warriors—formed based on the Oxygen Manifesto embrace eco-socialism. Though it is initially treated as a fringe idea by both the media and mainstream political parties, the Oxygen Manifesto would soon catch the imagination of common people.

Though the book's politics is deep, Misra's writing ensures that it is an easy read. And this book is a must-read for anyone who wonders what ordinary citizens can do to save Mother Earth.

Oxygen Manifesto—A Battle for Environment
Author: Atulya Misra
Publisher: Rupa Publications
Pages: 195
Price: ₹495

Fresh perspective

If art were a room, Prasoon Joshi would have explored every nook and cranny of it in his book *Thinking Aloud*. The book is a collection of essays in which he writes about topics as diverse as the growing violence on television, romance in Hindi cinema and the changing world of advertising. The tone is intelligent and incisive. Whether it is combining poetry and philosophy or decimating hierarchy in art forms, he imbues every topic with a vivid perspective. The great thing about *Thinking Aloud* is that it is not prescriptive. Rather, its vision is expansive, as Joshi acknowledges, and even exalts the existence of differences. "Is there a deficit of humility and grace," he asks, "to acknowledge that parallel narratives exist and must be engaged with, and not vociferously dismissed?" Amen to that.

Thinking Aloud Reflections on Emerging India
Author: Prasoon Joshi
Publisher: Rupa
Pages: 193
Price: ₹500

Tech-tonic changes

Where Will Man Take Us?
Author: Atul Jalan
Publisher: Penguin Random House
Pages: 272
Price: ₹399

Atul Jalan is fascinated by one thing—life-technology intersections. According to him, we are living in a unique age in which the biology we inherited is merging with the technology we have created. What is helming these changes are AI, genetic engineering, nanotechnology and quantum computing. The implications of each of them are elaborated in the book. To say they are wide-reaching would be an understatement. We will be able to create our ideal partner with all our likes and dislikes programmed in. Surveillance states will monitor everything from our pulses to our preferences. Have you ever wondered whether you and I are 'evolved Marios' in someone's game? Or whether data is going to be the next God? Wonder no more. Just go pick up a copy of the book.

SUNDAY SPECIAL — DT NEXT

AUTHOR INTERVIEW

Chennai, Sunday, May 12, 2019

BRIDGING THE WORLDS OF BUREAUCRACY, BIODIVERSITY

Atulya Misra's work of fiction titled Oxygen Manifesto focuses on one of the biggest challenges facing us today — environmental protection

■ HEMAMALINI VENKATRAMAN

Photo: V Naresh Kumar

Atulya Misra, Additional Chief Secretary to Government, Revenue and Disaster Management Department, Tamil Nadu, is on a mission. His experience as a seasoned bureaucrat for over a quarter of a century has now inspired a literary outpouring as many decades in the making. The work of fiction titled *Oxygen Manifesto* is his labour of love and a parable for the times that we live in — focussing on one of the biggest challenges facing us today — environmental protection.

Linking the past, present and the future through characters that seek to highlight everyday concerns about the ecosystem, Misra manages to touch upon various facets of our existence. His two central characters — Thatha, an odd man from More (Manipur), and Ravi Chandran Bose, an interloper who helps connect the dots are cut from the same cloth as Misra — and have an agenda to keep the 'greens' intact.

Speaking to *DT Next*, Misra opens up on the germ of an idea that flowered into this modern day manifesto for planet Earth. He begins, "I had written this book a year ago with the intention of it being a call to arms of sorts." The desire to pursue a doctorate on the subject of carbon footprint and its impact on the world had led Misra through the hallowed corridors of Anna University, for his second stint as a student. He recalls, "It was a difficult process — studying in a classroom filled with youngsters and embarking on painstaking research and meticulous calculations. Interestingly, like my varsity days, falling into a regimen helped me internalise the important aspects of learning." This stint in research laid the foundation for his book, seeding the thought for creating a positive impact on the environment with sustainability at its core.

The actual trigger for the writing process was pulled under unexpected circumstances. He tells us, "At a family dinner to celebrate my wedding anniversary, I ran into a friend, whose conversation left me curious. This multi-lingual gentleman lived many lives — from his roots in Tamil Nadu to the North East where he travelled for work to 'off the chart' locations such as Afghanistan, Burma, Czechoslovakia, Mongolia."

Misra draws our attention to a few historical fiction-like characteristics of his book including a tip of the hat to Netaji Subhash Chandra Bose saying, "Thatha's father and his family are said to have crossed over to the kingdom of Manipur, escorted by none other than Bose's Indian National Army (INA)."

The book, he says, is meant to "convey a sense of urgency as the story takes you on a cross country journey — involving trysts with cultures, traditions, and environments. The idea is to offer insights into lifestyles and ethos followed by people keen on keeping their ecosystems alive and kicking. "For instance, in the chapter 'The Trigger,' the posting of the protagonist Ravi launches him into exploration mode. The challenges relating to a fragile ecosystem troubles him. Issues such as global warming, mono-cropping, deforestation, desertification, groundwater depletion, the rapid pile-up of nuclear and other hazardous waste, impurities in the air, contamination of water sources, the endless heaps of urban waste and other environmental issues haunt him," he says.

Misra, the bureaucrat, channels his own journey into sustainability, through his characters. Be it minimalism, veganism or the rights of the citizenry in the form of pedestrian's rights, he has aimed at presenting nuggets of information in a format that is meant to enthuse readers into thinking and acting. Showing the door to drone inducing data points and statistics, Misra chooses to draw parallels with a time when simple harmonious living was the norm. Misra owes a major debt of gratitude to change makers and activists who have come before him. "Take for instance, 92-year-young Sunderlal Bahuguna, the epicentre of the Chipko movement in Reni village of Uttarakhand, who created such a huge impact and without any social media at that time. He went on to inspire millions to put in persistent efforts to plant trees over decades." With actioneers like Misra at hand, there still is hope to drive home a cohesive narrative of sustainability.

> "I had written this book a year ago with the intention of it being a call to arms of sorts"
> — Atulya Misra, Additional Chief Secretary